SPECIAL MESSAGE TO READERS

A LOVE WORTH WAITING FOR

In the lovely village of Manorbier in Pembrokeshire, Jasmine gets the opportunity to open up a teashop — her dream come true. However, disturbing events threaten her business prospects, forcing Jasmine to search her heart and discover who wants the teashop closed. Is it the controlling boyfriend she has put in the past? Or someone wanting the premises for himself . . . local artist Rhys Morgan, for instance? Jasmine has to put her heart on hold until the sinister campaign is over.

KAREN ABBOTT

A LOVE WORTH WAITING FOR

Complete and Unabridged

LINFORD
Leicester

First published in Great Britain in 2010

First Linford Edition
published 2010

British Library CIP Data

Abbott, Karen.
A love worth waiting for. - -
(Linford romance library)
1. Tearooms- -Fiction. 2. Businesswomen- -
Fiction. 3. Artists- -Fiction. 4. Pembrokeshire
(Wales)- -Social conditions- -Fiction.
5. Love stories 6. Large type books.
I. Title II. Series
823.9'2–dc22

ISBN 978–1–44480–450–8

Published by
F. A. Thorpe (Publishing)
Anstey, Leicestershire

Set by Words & Graphics Ltd.
Anstey, Leicestershire
Printed and bound in Great Britain by
T. J. International Ltd., Padstow, Cornwall

This book is printed on acid-free paper

1

Lowering the property supplement, Darys Williams called out, 'Hey, how about this one, Jaz? *High Street Café in excellent position, with recent improvements to equipment and decor. For sale or rent. 50 years lease remaining.* Sounds ideal, don't you think?'

'Too ideal!' Jasmine Jones demurred, chewing the end of her pencil. 'I can't afford the 'ideal position'! I need something in need of some tender, loving care in a not-your-first-choice position. Keep looking.'

'Sounds like you're looking for a lot of hard work!' Darys laughed.

'I don't mind hard work,' Jasmine countered, running her finger down a column of adverts in a rival newspaper. 'Energy and ideas, I have plenty of — it's money that's scarce. Now, this one sounds promising. *Small village store near Pembrokeshire coast. In need of refurbishment. Owner's permission necessary for any change of use. Viewing highly recommended.'*

Jasmine paused. 'Change of use, eh?' she pondered. 'That probably means a supermarket has opened nearby and pinched all their custom. Well, that's okay by me. I'm not wanting a general store.'

'But what if the owner doesn't want his property changed into a tea shop? It says 'permission necessary', don't forget.'

'I'll face that if and when the need arises. There's no photo, so it might be too much of a dump even for me to consider — but it's a possibility. Keep on looking, though. I want at least half a dozen properties to look at. I'm going to make the most of my week off work next week . . . and, who knows, The Grand Old Duke might have to learn to manage without me.'

'Carl won't like it!'

'I don't give a hoot! I told you; it's all

over. I finally told him last night.'

'What! You told him to sling his hook elsewhere?'

'Not in those words, exactly . . . but, yes, that was the general meaning.'

'Well, I hope you made it clear. You know what he's like. His inflated ego will convince him what you really mean is that you can't live without him!'

'Tough! I said it was final this time. I've had enough! I want to make my own decisions in life, not live in Carl's shadow or dance like a puppet.'

'Good for you! And moving to another area should make it harder for him to pester you to go back with him.'

By Wednesday lunchtime and three properties later, Jasmine wasn't feeling quite so optimistic. Two properties had been no-hopers and the third, although ideal in many ways, had no living accommodation and no space for conversion into such, so that, too, was crossed off the list.

'Right! Manorbier, here I come!' she promised out loud as she selected first gear of her Austin Mini and headed for the coast.

It was a lovely spring day and, as Jasmine turned off the trunk road, she had a sudden surge of optimism about the property she was about to view. It was the only one that stated it was near the coast and, surely, that was an ideal place for a new tea shop . . . as long as there wasn't already one in the village. A place this small couldn't support two, especially as the medieval castle on the outskirts of the village probably had its own tea room. She felt nervous, dreading the sudden sight of a thriving tea shop.

Her first glimpse of the bright blue sea cheered her. It looked as though someone had scattered handfuls of diamonds onto its surface and they twinkled merrily, dazzling in the sunshine. The road swung westwards, parallel to the rocky coast. She passed some houses, a post office, a hotel — with no sign of a tea garden, she noted in relief. Then, opposite a road that led to the castle and the access to the coast, she saw the small village store.

To make sure there wasn't a potential rival lurking round the corner, Jasmine drove past along the road out of the village, glancing left and right. No sign of any tea shops. Good! She turned her car around and returned to the centre of the village. Now for the village store!

It was standing almost apologetically at the end of a row of cottages at the curve of the village street. It had a small frontage, at present occupied by an old van, and its outer appearance agreed with its owner's assessment that it needed refurbishment. Its large front window was painted over in dark green, with the words 'Village Store' picked out in red. A smaller window to the left of the door was filled with a display of faded packaged goods.

Jasmine carefully manoeuvred her Mini into the remaining space and switched off the engine. What was the property like inside? The agent had told her that the owner was an elderly lady called Mrs Hughes, who was finding it difficult to continue due to failing health.

'But the property has been in her family for a number of generations and she's reluctant to sell it straight off. The place has character, apparently,' he added somewhat scathingly. 'She doesn't want it being used for anything she doesn't approve of. Doesn't want to *upset the village*. Huh! Old ladies, eh? Bats in the belfry, no doubt. So tread carefully. Make sure only positive vibes come through!'

What you saw was what you got, as far as Jasmine was concerned. She wasn't going to put on an act for anybody. If her face didn't fit, so be it.

She gathered up her bag, with notebook and pen. Mrs Hughes wasn't the only one to attach conditions.

Inside, it was like stepping back a hundred years. Lighting came from a couple of low-watt bulbs dangling from the ceiling. Attempts had been made to drag the store into the previous century by making it a self-service store, but the aisles were narrow, dark and crowded and the shelves only sparingly stocked with utilitarian commodities. The contents of the fresh fruit and vegetable section were indeed fresh, but again unimaginative. Apples, bananas, and pears; potatoes, carrots, onions and greens. Nothing to inspire anyone to be adventurous in the kitchen. She glanced around at the walls and ceiling. It was clean, but in need of redecoration.

'Can I help you, dear?'

Jasmine saw an elderly lady emerging from a doorway from the rear. She had a pleasant appearance; none of the eccentricity Jasmine had expected.

'Mrs Hughes? I'm Jasmine Jones. Mr Cadwallader, the estate agent, arranged an appointment for me this lunchtime.' She held out her hand as she spoke. 'I'm looking for a suitable property to rent for a new business I hope to set up.'

'And what sort of business would

that be, Miss Jones?' Mrs. Hughes asked as she gently took Jasmine's hand.

'A tea shop,' Jasmine said quickly, seeing no point in prevaricating. If Mrs Hughes didn't like the idea, she may as well know from the outset. 'A place where I will sell my own home-baked goods, and do light lunches and afternoon teas,' she hurried on. 'I've looked around and there's no other such place in the vicinity and, well, I hoped . . . '

Her voice tailed off and she looked helplessly at the elderly owner.

'Would you like to look around the property?' Mrs Hughes asked, her voice friendly but not betraying her inner thoughts.

'Yes, please,' Jasmine agreed, meekly following her into the rear part of the building.

The kitchen had an old-fashioned range and a central table; the walls were lined with cupboards, which, although not exactly modern, would serve their purpose for the time being; and a double-drainer sink was situated under the window that overlooked a small yard. A doorway led into a short passage running from the front to the rear, with a toilet and separate bathroom looking on to the back yard. Across the passage was a door into a small living room, which overlooked a small rear garden — and another door that, surprisingly, led back into the shop, into the part that held a small selection of kitchenware, hardware and outside goods. That room, in turn, led back into the main store.

'What a lot of doors!' Jasmine laughed. 'You could get quite dizzy running round through them all!'

'Which we did, as children!' Mrs Hughes agreed with a smile. 'Hide and seek and tag. What a time we had! It was like living in a treasure house, though we weren't allowed to touch any of the goods for sale, of course.'

Jasmine found a mixture of emotions welling up inside her as they continued the tour of the living quarters, mounting the narrow staircase that led onto a small landing with doors leading into three good-sized bedrooms. She loved the place — the store, which she could already visualise as her tea room; the living quarters; and its position in such a lovely village with its vibrant historic past, including one of the best mediaeval castles of Wales. But the size of the living quarters was disquieting her. She only needed something half its size . . . could only *afford* something about half its size.

When they descended the staircase again and Mrs Hughes said, 'Now, what do you think, dear?' Jasmine knew her voice betrayed her anxiety when she replied, 'I love it — but what sort of rental will you be asking?'

When Mrs Hughes named the amount she was asking each month, Jasmine felt thoroughly deflated. It was almost twice as much as she could afford. She had discussed her plans with her bank manager and he had demanded a detailed forecast to cover any renovations and decorating that might be required — and this property would need the upper limit of her forecast. Mr Pritchard had given her a definite limit that could be loaned against any property. The words 'a young woman of your tender years' had figured somewhere in his discourse. How would he react if she returned to his office with a request for a larger loan? She could but try. It was either that or start searching again — and with this property now her ideal, how would she rate anything else?

'I really do like it, Mrs Hughes,' she began.

'Oh, call me Lona, dear. It's short for Maelona. It means 'princess' in Welsh, you know. My dada's little princess, I was . . . many years ago now.'

'Right, er, Lona. Well, as I said, I really do like it, but it's more than I can afford at the moment. You couldn't drop your price a little, could you?'

'I'd love to, Miss Jones . . . Jasmine

. . . but my son is furious enough with me as it is. He thought I should just hand it over to him and let him do as he wants with it. But I said, 'No. I need the money to finance my retirement.' Which is true, so I can't let it go for less. I'm sorry, dear. I really feel you would be the ideal person. You fit in here, somehow.'

Jasmine nodded sadly. 'I understand . . . and I have two more properties to view.' She cast her eyes around, loving every nook and cranny. It had character, life and a good feeling for the future.

'I'll have to think about it,' she temporised, not wanting to give a definite 'no'. 'Maybe my bank manager will agree to lending me more when I tell him what a find it is?'

'Well, you phone me and let me know how you get on,' Lona said cheerfully. 'If you're meant to have it, it will be yours somehow.'

And, on that optimistic note, Jasmine bade her farewell.

* * *

Jasmine spent the next two days viewing the other properties but, as she suspected, neither lived up to the prospects of the village store at Manorbier. A hastily arranged interview with Mr Pritchard drew a blank.

Jasmine returned to the flat she shared with Darys to share her dismal news. 'I'd better phone Mrs Hughes and tell her I'm out of the picture,' she concluded with a heavy sigh. 'And then I'll have to start all over again.'

Mrs Hughes answered promptly and listened without comment as Jasmine sorrowfully outlined her failure to come up with the necessary amount of money.

'Now, my dear, I may have an answer to your quandary,' she said when Jasmine's voice tailed away. 'Why don't you come here tomorrow at, shall we say, one-thirty? I close at one o'clock on Saturdays out of season so we'll be able to talk undisturbed by any customers, won't we?'

'I'm not sure it will be worth taking up your time,' Jasmine apologised.

'Now don't decide until you hear what I have to say,' Mrs Hughes remonstrated. 'So, I'll see you tomorrow, eh? Half-past one!'

Why not? Jasmine thought. She had nothing to lose. 'Yes, all right then. I'll see you tomorrow.'

* * *

Rhys Morgan hit the edge of the steering wheel of his battered Bedford van with the heel of his hand in a mixture of resignation, frustration and despair. Cilla couldn't die on him now! She mustn't! But, as the van's engine coughed, spluttered and faded into silence, he knew that she had.

He steered the lifeless hunk of rust-on-wheels into the gateway of a field and sent a small prayer heavenward that no-one would need access to the field before he'd had time to summon assistance. He'd noticed the temperature gauge rising steadily yesterday and signs of steam escaping from the radiator earlier today. He should have stopped earlier when he was on the main road. At least there was more passing traffic there, and more chance of getting a lift. He glanced at his watch, thankful that he'd allowed plenty of time, but with the best will in the world he couldn't manage to jog five or six miles in much less than two hours, which meant he would be late.

He locked the van door, though he doubted anyone would be foolish enough to steal it — they'd be doing him a favour if they did! Apart from all the paperwork, that is — and the loss of the few personal possessions he carried with him. Now, was there at least one generous-minded driver who wouldn't have an aversion to offering a lift to a lone young man?

The first two cars passed without even slowing down, so, when he saw an old Mini approaching at a more sedate pace, he decided to make a bolder effort to draw attention to his predicament. With little regard to safety, he stepped out into the road and flapped his arms up and down, trying to look desperately in need of a lift. For a heart-stopping moment he thought the driver hadn't seen him and he tensed the muscles of his legs ready to leap aside — but at the last moment the driver, a young woman whose startled face was framed by short blonde curls, slammed on the brakes and stopped with only inches to spare.

Rhys dropped his hands onto the edge of the bonnet and tried not to look as frightened as he felt as they glared at each other through the windshield. His heart was beating fast with the rush of adrenalin. He had really thought the driver was about to run him down!

The woman yanked on the handbrake, switched off the engine and opened the car door.

'Are you crazy?' she yelled at him, eyes blazing. 'Are you tired of living and too scared to jump off a cliff?'

Rhys stared at her. She really was the most gorgeous girl he had met in ages — or ever, he reconsidered — especially with her eyes blazing like that. They were as blue as a summer sky on a cloudless day.

'Well?' she demanded, obviously not as impressed with him as he was with her. The girl came nearer and stood with her hands on her hips.

'I'm really sorry!' he apologised meekly. 'It's just that I was desperate.'

'Desperate for what?'

'A lift. My van's broken down.' He gestured behind him. 'That heap of useless metal! She spluttered and died on me just when I needed her most.'

'Huh! Just like you treat all females, I suppose? Maybe all it needed was a bit of TLC. My car's just as old as your van and it's perfectly reliable!'

'You might have a point. I did know she needed some attention, but I've been busy. I meant to get her fixed after her service next week. She's never let me down before. A grand old girl, is Cilla!'

'Cilla! What sort of name is that for a car?' the girl snorted.

'Sorry,' he apologised again, thinking he'd better work fast to put on some charm. 'It's her registration number. See . . . CLA . . . CILLA. And, besides, Cilla Black was one of my gran's favourite singers back in the sixties, and she helped me buy the van for my twenty-first.'

'Huh,' the girl said again, but with less force. 'So, where are you going? Or hoping to go?'

'Just as far as Manorbier,' Rhys told her. 'It's not far. Or, just as far as the A4139, if you prefer. I could get another lift from there.'

'You mightn't survive your next attempt! Get in. I'm going there myself.'

She swung back towards the driver's side of her car and climbed in, leaning across to open the passenger door. Rhys sank onto the seat.

'Thanks. I really am grateful. You lone women can't be too careful these days, I know, so I'm doubly grateful.'

The girl paused in the action of starting up the engine and eyed him with renewed hostility. 'Do you want this lift, or don't you?'

'Huh? What did I say?'

'We live in a world of so-called equality. Or don't you think so?'

'Yeah. Sure. Women are just as good as men — at some things.'

'Some?' She glared.

'Most. It depends on whether you're talking brain or brawn, doesn't it? Anyway, what is it with you? Some man trodden on your toes or something? If so, and you promise to start that engine, I'll get him back. What shall I do? Thump him or trip him up?'

'You're at it again!' she reprimanded him more lightly, reaching out to switch on the engine. 'I'll deal with him myself, probably by changing my bank. Fasten your seatbelt. We're off!'

'Ah, bank manager, eh?' He clunk-clicked. 'If it's any consolation, I've had a run-in with one of those myself, and I'm a bloke!'

'Glad to hear it!' she grinned. 'That you're a bloke, I mean — not that your bank manager turned you down. What was his excuse? Mine couched it in terms of my youth and lack of experience, but I could tell he meant it was because I'm female.'

'Huh! Almost word for word! He didn't exactly turn me down but he put a low limit on what he was prepared to lend. If you ask me, it's an age thing. I wouldn't call him an old fogey, but he's definitely the wrong side of fifty.'

'Whereas we twenty-somethings are in the prime of our lives and should be given all the encouragement we need.'

'Exactly! I couldn't agree more.'

Their eyes met briefly in smiling, mutual agreement. Rhys felt a stirring deep within him and he realised he wanted to get know her better. They were descending down the hill towards the centre of Manorbier village and he knew he would have to work fast. He glanced at his watch.

'Thanks for your lift. I've now got nearly an hour to spare. D'you fancy a spot of lunch somewhere? There's no café, as far as I know, but I'm sure this hotel on the left will do light lunches.'

'What time is it now?'

'Twelve thirty-five.'

Rhys could see she was tempted by his offer. Maybe she thought he couldn't afford it? 'Take it as my way of saying 'thanks for the lift' — and it would give me a great deal of pleasure.'

She smiled warmly at him. 'Okay. Just a snack, though. I have an appointment to keep later.'

'Yes, me, too.'

She pulled off the road and parked the car quite niftily for a woman, although he decided not to say so. Instead, he waited until she had locked her door and joined him to walk into the hotel.

'By the way, my name's Rhys . . .

Rhys Morgan.' He held out his hand.

'Nice to know you, Rhys. And I'm Jasmine. Jasmine Jones.'

Again, they smiled in mutual companionship and walked into the hotel like old friends. After glancing at the pricey menu, they agreed to have the soup of the day with a bread roll. Rhys liked her all the more for that. Many a girl would have gone for the most expensive item on the menu.

'What do you do for your living?' he asked as they waited for the soup to be brought to their table.

'I'm one of the assistant chefs at the Duke of York Hotel in Cardigan. And what about you?'

'I work at a leisure complex near Carmarthen — but, mostly, I paint.'

'Pictures or decorating?'

'Which d'you think?'

She considered him closely, making his heart leap about again.

'Mmmm. Probably pictures.'

'Spot on!'

The time flew by. Before Rhys knew

it, Jasmine was wiping her rosy lips on her napkin and picking up her keys.

'Time to go, I'm afraid. Thanks for lunch. I've really enjoyed meeting you.'

'My pleasure. Here . . . ' He felt in his pocket and pulled out a scrap of paper and a pen. 'Here's my phone number. Give me a call sometime, eh?'

Jasmine took it. 'I'll give you mine.'

'That's okay. You ring me . . . equality and all that.'

She laughed. 'Right! D'you want a lift to where you're going?'

'No, it's not far. I'll settle up here and walk down.'

She walked to the door and glanced back over her shoulder, as Rhys knew she would. 'Don't forget to ring me!' he called.

'I won't. See you!'

Rhys watched her go, hoping she meant it.

2

Driving down the hill, Jasmine indicated right and turned into the small parking space at the side of the village store. She glanced at her watch. Twenty-five past one. Good. She was a little early.

She felt quite nervous, wondering what Lona Hughes had in mind. Was she prepared to drop her rental price? It was the only thing that made any sense of asking her to come back to discuss matters. But would she drop it far enough? Mr Pritchard had been adamant about the size of her allowed overdraft for renovations, and even that depended on a surveyor's report.

The door to the store was locked and the 'Closed' sign in place, so Jasmine pressed the bell-push and waited, glancing around at the shop's exterior. The stonework seemed in reasonable condition, but the wooden window frames and door might need to be renewed, and the fascia boards — and she would need tables and chairs for indoors and out. And a few parasols. No — she mustn't let her imagination start to move on until she knew what Mrs Hughes had to say.

The door opened, and the warmth of welcome in Lona Hughes's eyes both bewildered and excited her. Had she been clear enough about not being able to afford the rent?

'Come on in, dearie. I've got the kettle on. Go through to the living-room. You remember where it is?'

She did. She remembered every inch of the place.

She stepped into the store, leaving Lona to close the door behind them. The elderly lady glanced left and right along the village street. Was she expecting someone else? Maybe the son she'd mentioned? Whatever, Lona closed the door and ushered Jasmine through the store and kitchen and across the passageway into the living room, chattering inconsequentially about the bright spring weather.

'Make yourself at home, dear, while I brew the tea. Have you had lunch? You have? How about a custard tart or a scone, then? I've got some ready.'

She bustled back to the kitchen and, left alone, Jasmine leaned back against the cushions on the sofa, letting her glance sweep around the room. She would have loved it here, she knew she would. There was something about the ambience of the place. Even though she knew she would have been radically altering the interior of the store, she'd have kept its basic structure and retained many of its timeless fittings. Oh, if only . . . But life wasn't built on if-onlies. She must be prepared to move on.

Lona carried in a tea tray loaded with custard tarts, fruit tarts and scones; a teapot, milk jug and a pile of cups and saucers — three of each, Jasmine noticed. So she *was* expecting someone!

Did her son want to stake his claim to the property and tell her that her dreams were mere moonshine?

Lona must have sensed her speculation and she began to speak as she poured the milk and tea into two of the cups.

'I expect you're wondering why I asked you to come back today. The fact is, I had another interested viewer on Thursday. I quite took to him and liked his proposed change-of-usage for the property.'

'Oh.' Jasmine's face fell.

So, that's the way it was, was it? She was disappointed in the elderly woman. She hadn't put her down as someone who would play off one against another. Maybe her son had suggested it as a way to boost the rental price — a sort of mini-auction? Too bad! Even if she were willing to play the game, which she wasn't, she couldn't do so unless she won the lottery. And that would be impossible since she never played it.

She withdrew her hand from the cup

she was about to accept.

'I'm sorry. As I said on the phone last night, I really can't afford to meet your price, let alone raise it. I'd love to, I really would, but it's impossible and I really don't want to waste your time.'

She made as if to get up from the sofa but Lona waved her hand.

'No, you're not wasting my time. You've misunderstood what I'm trying to say. The other viewer . . .'

The doorbell rang and Lona got up from her chair.

'Ah, that's him now, I expect. Help yourself, dear, while I let him in.'

Jasmine looked at the tempting array but she didn't feel like eating. The food would stick in her throat, she was sure. The sound of voices drawing nearer heralded Lona's return with the other prospective tenant and Jasmine frowned as she heard the second voice. It was male, fairly young, and somewhat familiar. Surely not?

'In the living room, Rhys,' she heard Lona say, confirming her thoughts. And so it was no surprise when Rhys Morgan entered the room.

'Hi! I knew it must be you!' he exclaimed in greeting, grinning broadly, as if he expected her to be pleased to meet him as a competitor.

He was holding out his hand but Jasmine ignored it.

'You knew!' she said coldly. 'Then why all that friendly talk and buying my lunch? Were you hoping to soften me up and make me feel sorry for you so I'd withdraw from the scene and leave the way clear for you? Well, you needn't have bothered. I can't afford it, anyway!'

'No, no — I only meant I knew it was you when I saw your car outside.'

'You know each other?' Lona asked. 'That makes my plan all the better!'

'Hardly!' Jasmine snapped, replying to Lona's first four words. She scowled at Rhys, disclaiming any pretext of friendship between them. 'Of all the low tricks . . .'

'What plan?' Rhys asked Lona, not

heeding Jasmine's scorn.

Lona looked at him and then at Jasmine. 'I think we need to start again.'

'There's no point. I can't afford it,' Jasmine stated flatly, all fight draining out of her.

'Neither can I,' Rhys agreed. 'So, what's your plan, Mrs Hughes?'

'Call me Lona, dear.' She smiled from one to the other. 'No, neither of you can afford to rent this property separately — but, together, you can!'

'Together?' both echoed, looking at each other and then back at Lona.

'Impossible!' Jasmine snapped, still feeling that, somehow, Rhys had put her at a disadvantage.

'Hang on. Let's hear what Lona has to say,' Rhys invited, sitting down next to Jasmine on the sofa. Jasmine drew herself away slightly, distancing herself from Rhys and his open enthusiasm.

Lona smiled. 'Well, as I see it, you both want to start a new business and both need somewhere about half the size of this property at half the cost. Am I right?'

Both nodded; Rhys eagerly, Jasmine with more reluctance. She didn't want someone sorting out her problems and making her decisions. That's what Carl did; she'd had enough of that.

'Well, let's think about it, shall we? The passageway out there,' Lona suggested, nodding towards the door, 'cuts the ground floor neatly in half. You, Rhys, could have the annexe of the shop as your selling space — your gallery, I expect you'll call it — and this room for whatever else you need, storage or living space or a mixture of both. Jasmine will have the main store for her tea room and the kitchen as her workplace. You could share the facilities in there for your personal use, I'm sure, and the bathroom would have to be shared, too, but I'm sure you'll manage that without any problems. You young people today have a much more relaxed idea about such things than in my day. Good heavens! A man and a woman had to be engaged before they were allowed to walk out together!'

She laughed at the incredible changes that had come about in her lifetime, then smiled, looking to see how her ideas were being received.

Jasmine kept her face impassive. She felt she was being hustled along a route that she hadn't thought about. Had they already worked it out between them? Was she being set up in any way?

She glanced at Rhys. His face was more receptive. He was smiling and nodding as Lona resumed expressing her thoughts.

'Now, as you know, there are three bedrooms. The one above the annexe is lovely and light and would make an ideal studio to paint in. The light comes in from both sides, so Rhys ought to have that. And maybe Jasmine could choose which of the other two rooms she'd like as her bedroom?'

She sat back and placed her hands in her lap.

'There! Now, what do you think?

Why don't you have a wander around as you consider what I've suggested? We would draw up a mutually agreed legal contract between us, and I'd be willing to put a share into the costs of any improvements that are made to the actual structure of the property.'

Jasmine had to admit it sounded a reasonable deal — but she didn't want to say so immediately. She needed time to think about it. The other two were looking at her expectantly. She reached for the cup of tea and sipped it, thinking furiously.

'It could work, I suppose,' she said tentatively. 'But, as you say, we need time to consider what you've suggested.'

She didn't want her thoughts muddled by Rhys and his all-too-obvious enthusiasm for the plan. The mutual chemistry between them was strong. She could feel her heart beating erratically and her pulse racing at his closeness . . . or was it her nervousness at considering the change of her plans? For that reason alone, was it going to be a good idea to share the property? She didn't want to get sidetracked from her business idea. On the other hand, if they got on well together, that would make a working/living relationship run more smoothly.

She replaced her cup and saucer on the table. 'I'll wander around for a while, like you said. Separately,' she added sternly, as Rhys leaped to his feet. 'I'll start upstairs.'

'Right you are. I'll start down here,' Rhys said agreeably. 'Thanks for the tea, Lona. I'll munch a scone as I go, if that's all right.'

'I'll leave them on the table. Give me a shout if you need to ask me anything at all, my dears. I'll just be out in the back garden.'

Jasmine made her way upstairs. The stairs cut the upper floor in half, the back from the front, with the proposed studio and the other front room on the same stretch of landing. That made it more sensible for her to have the smaller back room. Would she be happy with that? It wasn't ideal, but she could live with it. She'd spend most of her time in the kitchen and tea room. The medium-sized front room was pleasant and would make a better bedsit.

What about the proposed studio? She went into it. It was light and airy, much lighter than the other front room. Lona was right about that. If Rhys had that and the adjacent room as his bedroom, that might give her some bargaining power to persuade him to allow her to have some tables on the pavement in front of his window.

She went downstairs, meeting Rhys waiting to go up.

'What d'you think?' he asked.

'Mmm,' she murmured non-committally. 'The upstairs division needs some consideration. See what you think.'

She went into the store and mentally blocked out all the shelving and display stands. She'd need a display cabinet for sandwiches, pies and pastries, probably near the door into the kitchen. She'd have the till there, too. It would be more secure, rather than at the door where Lona had it. As for the rest of the space . . . She half-closed her eyes and assessed the size of the room. Six or seven tables for four, she reckoned; or maybe one or two of them for two, with another two or three outside, that would give her seating for between thirty and forty at maximum, probably fewer in reality. She'd have to build up her custom and take on extra help.

Would it work? It could; she knew it could. It would mean a bit of compromise, but Rhys seemed agreeable. Right! Time for discussion.

Rhys was on his way downstairs.

'What d'you think?' he asked again. 'Are you ready to discuss it? Or do you need more time to think about it?'

She smiled brightly. 'No, I'm ready to discuss it right now. One thing before we start. Did you know about Lona's plan when we met earlier?'

'No. It was as new to me as it was to you. Lona had said someone else was interested but she hadn't said anything about you.' He appraised her stance and wondered if he would have his work cut out trying to persuade her to give it a try. 'So, what's your overall feeling? Is it feasible or not?'

Jasmine took a deep breath. 'It's feasible,' she agreed lightly.

'Good! I think so, too. Let's discuss who has what, then.'

'Right. Well, I thought that the two front rooms seem to belong to each other, since they're on the same part of the landing. The biggest, as Lona said, would make a better studio so I'm willing to have the smaller one.'

Rhys was surprised that she was being so generous. 'That won't give you much space to relax in, though, will it?'

'Maybe not, but the other is definitely better as your studio.'

'I agree, but I'm willing to have it double as my bedroom. I don't need anything fancy and there's plenty of room for a single bed, which can also double as a sofa. That would give you a bedroom and a sitting room.'

'Oh!' It took away her bargaining

power for the tables outside. Still, it would be really nice to have two rooms. She nodded. 'I'll go with that.'

'Good! Is Lona's suggested plan for downstairs to your liking?'

'Yes, it's fine. You'll have a sitting room there and obviously we'll share the kitchen and bathroom.'

'Great! Let's call Lona inside and we'll get our leases sorted!'

Lona was delighted that they had reached agreement.

'I'm sure you'll get on very well together. Now, there's a lot to do. We'll need to get all the legalities sorted as soon as possible and I'll put a Closing Down Sale notice in my window for, shall we say, the Easter weekend?'

'Won't the villagers miss your store?' Jasmine asked.

'Good gracious, no. Most of them go to the big supermarkets, and the local postmaster is planning to extend his business by diversifying into general goods. We've only been waiting for the right people to come along and I'm sure that's you two. Now, you both need to seek planning permission for the change of usage and any alterations you want to make. You shouldn't have any problems, I've already made enquiries about that. So, let's shake on it, shall we?'

Which they did.

Jasmine felt a frisson of delight pass through her when Rhys took hold of her hand. He didn't say anything but his eyes seemed to convey that their touch meant something to him as well.

He smiled. 'Jasmine?'

Her heart leapt. 'Yes?'

'May I beg a lift back as far as my van?'

'Oh.' That deflated her a little. 'Sure.'

She turned to Lona Hughes. 'Goodbye for now, Lona. I'll be in touch.'

'We all will, dear. I've got your phone numbers.'

Back at Rhys's van, he shook his head when it failed to start and got out his mobile phone. 'I'll get my local garage to come out and take it in.'

Jasmine waited while he made the call.

'Not until after five?' she heard him query. 'Sure. Yes, that's okay. I'll be here waiting.'

'Can I give you a lift somewhere?' she asked. 'That means you've over two hours to wait.'

'Thanks, but no. I'll be okay. I'll do some sketching, I've got all I need in the back of my van. If I cross this field, I should be able to see the coast. It's an artist's paradise round here.'

'Right.' She held out her hand. 'I'll look forward to seeing you again, then, Rhys.'

'Me, too,' he agreed. 'So long, then.'

Jasmine drove away with mixed emotions . . . an inner excitement at the thought of the plans for her tea shop, a sense of promise for her working relationship with Rhys and a heartfelt hope that she had made the right decision.

She looked in her rear view mirror, wondering if Rhys would be watching her until she drove out of sight. She was slightly disappointed that he wasn't. He was delving into the back of his van, no doubt having forgotten all about her already.

He hadn't. He was getting out his sketchpad and pencil, but it wasn't the local scenery he began to pencil in. It was a girl's face with her eyes alight with an inner vision and her fair hair blown back by the breeze.

3

'Before I forget, Carl called round,' Darys informed Jasmine after she had shared what had transpired in Manorbier.

'Oh. What did you tell him?'

'Just what you said the other day, that it was over and you meant it this time. He said he wants to hear it from you and will call back sometime.'

Jasmine sighed. She had gone through all this before and had been persuaded to give it another go. 'Why can't he just accept it's over?' she moaned. 'What does he want? A huge row to convince him I mean it?'

'Probably — and then some! He likes to be the one who does the dumping; not the other way round.'

'He can tell people he dumped me, if that's what he prefers. I don't care. Anyway, I'm handing in my notice on

Monday. He can say we just drifted apart, if it soothes his ego.'

'Ha! It'll take more than that. Tell him you've got a new bloke, such as this Rhys you're sharing the premises with. He'll have to accept it then.'

Jasmine's shoulders sagged. 'Why should I have to lie to get him off my back? And I don't want to use Rhys in that way. Things like that have a habit of rebounding on you!'

'And you think it might come true?' Darys asked with a sly grin.

Jasmine threw a cushion at her. 'No.'

Darys caught it and threw it back. 'Not even a teensy-weensy little bit?'

Jasmine felt her cheeks warm. 'He's nice,' she temporised, 'but I want to get my tea shop up and running without the complication of getting caught up in another relationship — especially with Rhys. If we started something and it didn't work out, it could make things a bit awkward. Best to keep it as a working relationship.'

'Hmm! We'll see!' Darys murmured sagely.

Half an hour later, the phone rang. Darys groaned and rolled her eyes when she heard Jasmine agreeing to meet Carl in town for a friendly drink.

'Shall I come with you?' she offered. 'James won't mind us meeting up a little late in such a good cause.'

Jasmine shook her head. 'No, I'd rather do it on my own. No point in making it worse for Carl. He'd hate to have witnesses.'

Yet witnesses were just what Carl did want, apparently. When Jasmine arrived at the agreed venue, she discovered half a dozen other couples from the hotel where they worked gathered in the popular bar.

'Ah, there you are, Jaz!' Carl called out as she entered the bar.

He'd done it deliberately, Jasmine knew. He was counting on her going along the easier route of compliance. She hesitated as the rest of the crowd shuffled their seats to make room for her. Carl knew she hated scenes — and he was skilled at manipulation, as she had learned to her cost through the duration of their relationship. Aware that her hesitation was drawing attention to herself, she slipped into place beside Carl, her smile of greeting to the others feeling as tight-lipped as it no-doubt looked.

'We need to talk!' she hissed in his ear.

'Sure we do!' he agreed lightly. 'I was just saying to the others that you're the ideal person to take over as honorary president of our social group now that Louise is leaving. I'll be right there with you as back-up and Jack's agreed to be secretary, haven't you, Jack?'

'Yeah, great!' Jack agreed, lifting his tankard of beer. 'Here's to our new president! Long may she reign!'

Murmurs of agreement sounded around the group and, with all eyes upon her, Jasmine knew she had to make her move now or she'd be swamped by everyone else's enthusiasm.

'I'm honoured,' she began tentatively, 'but I must decline.' She glanced around with an apologetic smile, but her glance rested mainly on Carl. 'I'll be handing in my notice on Monday. I'm moving on!'

'Hey! You're a dark horse!'

'Aw, we'll miss you!'

'Where are you going?'

Various comments flowed from her colleagues, but the narrowing of Carl's eyes stilled them all. He knocked back his drink in a single gulp as he gripped Jasmine's elbow with his left hand and hauled her to her feet. He placed his glass on the table with studied calm.

'Sorry, folks. We need a minute alone. We'll catch up with you all later when I've talked some sense into this little tease.'

Jasmine felt unable to protest as he hustled her away from their corner of the bar, through the crowd and out into the street, but tried to wrest her arm free once they were out of public gaze.

'Let go of me, Carl! You're hurting

my arm!' she objected.

Carl continued to hustle her along the street until they were in a secluded doorway of a closed store.

'Don't you dare do that to me again!' he snarled, ignoring her cry as the back of her head struck the door. 'Everyone knows we're an item. How am I supposed to feel when you drop a bombshell like that? They all knew I hadn't a clue! You did it deliberately to humiliate me!'

'No, I didn't!' She shook her arms free of his grip and was relieved when he stepped back a little. She glared at him furiously. 'You set me up, there! You thought I'd go along with what you were saying because I wouldn't want to cause a fuss. Well, I'm not going to be pushed around by you any longer. You said you wanted to talk. Well, now we're talking, so listen to what I'm saying. I meant what I said last week. We're through . . . for good! Get it? Watch my lips if you're not sure. We're — through!'

Jasmine felt exhausted by her spurt of anger. She was thankful that Carl, though still clearly angry, now stood silently in front of her. 'I'm sorry it had to come to this, but you wouldn't listen.'

'But we're good together. Everybody says so. We *belong* to each other!'

'No, we don't. I don't belong to anyone. I'm a free agent, and I'm moving on. Like I said, I'm handing in my notice on Monday.'

'You can't move away! Where will you go? It's not easy to get a job in a hotel as good as the Grand Old Duke. Tell you what, I'll drop a hint to old Halston. He might offer you a rise. You'd stay for more pay, wouldn't you?'

Jasmine shook her head. 'No, actually I wouldn't. I already know what I'll be doing when I go.'

'And what's that?'

Jasmine didn't want to say. Manorbier was far enough away for the break to be final, and she didn't want him to know where she'd be living.

'Nothing's settled yet, but I know what sort of thing I want to do.' She straightened her posture and faced him candidly. 'Look, there's no point continuing like this. I'm determined to leave and nothing you say will persuade me otherwise. You can tell the others whatever you like. Tell them you're fed up with me . . . whatever . . . I'll go along with it. Now, if you don't mind, I'm going home. I'll see you around. No hard feelings, eh?'

She slipped past him. Carl tried to restrain her but she eluded his grasp. A group of people were coming along the street and, after a futile attempt to catch hold of her arm, Carl accepted the inevitable and Jasmine hurried away, thankful that she had parked her car not far away.

She sank into the driving seat and locked the door, just in case Carl had taken it into his head to follow her, but, when she looked around, there was no sign of him. She realised she was shaking. She needed to get home, have a hot bath and a comforting mug of hot chocolate. At least she would have the flat to herself, and by the time she'd be telling Darys about it tomorrow, she would be more composed.

She sighed with relief. It was over! She'd done it!

She was ready to move on.

* * *

The next two weeks at work were hard going as Carl fluctuated between coldly ignoring her presence, making sarcastic snide remarks when his audience was deemed sympathetic to his cause, and attempts to persuade her to reconsider her decision if they were alone.

'Look, you can still leave if you want. We could both do with a change,' he suggested one day. 'I'll come with you. Make a new start together.'

'No, Carl. I don't want that. I've already told you, I'm going on my own.'

'At least tell me where you're going. We can still be friends, can't we?'

'That's not a good idea. It wouldn't work.'

'Oh, for goodness' sake! What d'you think I am? I suppose you think I'd keep pestering you?'

And that was the trouble. She did think that — and, during one of her journeys to Manorbier, she felt sure she was being followed. A dark-coloured car drove behind her for many miles, and it was only when she was on the outskirts of Haverfordwest and dodged through a car park and out of the other side that she managed to lose it. Another time, it was a leather-clad motorcyclist who seemed to stay on her tail for many miles but, when she pulled into the forecourt of a garage, the motorcyclist swept by without a backward glance and she berated herself for being paranoid.

As Lona had predicted, the legal side sailed through all its stages and the only objection to the opening of a tea shop in the village came from the local hotel. The objection was mildly worded, since they catered mainly for a more up-market clientele.

'You're bound to steal some clients from the hotel,' Lona commented as she handed Jasmine a plate of bara brith. 'They'll be enticed in here for morning coffee or afternoon tea — but, on the other hand, other day-trippers, having had afternoon tea here, might decide to stay in the area for longer and call in at the hotel for an evening meal. Now, when do you plan to start arranging the alterations you want to make?'

'As soon as possible, really. I only had to work two weeks' notice because I took the rest of the time in holidays owing to me. Getting rid of your shelving will be my first task.'

'And that's no problem, dear. Marjorie from the post office said she's willing to take any you don't need off your hands.'

'Oh, great! I'll ask Rhys if he wants any for displaying his goods and, if not, Marjorie can have them. I just thought

I'd keep a couple for near the door, to display a few sidelines like packets of local sweets, biscuits, postcards and small souvenirs.'

Rhys didn't want the shop fittings. He planned to display any goods on rustic-style shelving — rough-hewn planks smoothed at the edges, supported by equally rough-hewn side pieces or even knotted rope wherever possible.

Once things were under way, Lona moved to her new apartment in Tenby and Jasmine decided to 'camp' in her designated bedroom to cut down on travelling time. It also meant she was further away from Carl and wouldn't need to worry about whether he was following her.

An easy working relationship had developed between her and Rhys. At first, he came and went as he fancied, but gradually he stayed more and more. When his studio was ready to be painted, a single divan bed was delivered and he became a permanent fixture.

'This is all I need,' he commented to Jasmine, indicating the few bits of furniture he'd brought. 'Lona's decided to start off with everything new in her apartment, so she's let me have all the stuff in the sitting room, plus one of the wardrobes. What about you?'

'Mum and Dad are letting me have things from my bedroom at home, so I just need a few things for my sitting room — a sofa, table and a few chairs. Second-hand will do, so I'll be touring junk shops when I have a free day. Darys is coming with me. She's good at getting prices down!'

Her progress was held up slightly when some damaged plaster fell at the far end wall of the store when the shelving there was removed. Lona engaged a surveyor, who pronounced the wall in need of repointing outside. Once that was done, and the inside wall cleared of remaining plaster, Jasmine decided the stonework made an effective complement to the plainness of the other walls and simply had it repointed.

The extra work put her slightly behind Rhys's progress with his renovations, but she drew level when Rhys toyed with the idea of lining the walls of his gallery with tongue-and-groove panelling but chose the cheaper option of painted plaster. Once the plaster was dry, they visited the nearest DIY store to buy large cans of paint and other decorating equipment.

A fresh coat of paint was all the upstairs rooms needed and then, with some cheap carpeting laid, Jasmine knew she would be able to move in properly. They had studied a number of colour charts together and both favoured pale, natural colours, so their selections were swiftly made.

'We'll use my van,' Rhys offered. 'We'll get everything we need in it, even a couple of short step-ladders.'

Dressed in old jeans and a much-worn sweater, Jasmine nodded her agreement, excited that the work was progressing so well and glad to follow Rhys' lead when it came to choosing the materials they needed.

The next few days saw them both hard at work. Jasmine decided to do her bedroom first so that any mistakes would be in her private domain. Painting ceilings was hardest, she decided, as she backed down the stepladder once more, removed the tray of paint from the top step and dragged the steps to a new position so that she could paint the next section.

'Oops!'

She'd forgotten she'd put the paint tray there and ruefully looked down at her right foot, now half-submerged in white emulsion. The roller had flipped over the side and lay in its own small pool of paint. Hmm! Well, she'd needed new carpet, anyway, so that didn't matter! Wiping the paint off her shoe took longer than expected and it was now a different shade from its partner. Maybe she'd better try to wash it off. She glanced at her watch. She'd pop the kettle on while she was down there.

'How's it going?' Rhys asked as she

entered the kitchen. 'I thought I'd have a coffee while I wash the roller. Want one?' He grinned broadly at her.

'Yes, please . . . and it's going fine, thanks.' She hid her shoe behind her back. 'Er, I'll be back in a minute!'

She scuttled out of the kitchen and along to the bathroom, glancing at the mirror as she passed. Her steps faltered and she backed up a pace. Her hair looked as if she had aged in the past hour, speckled as it was with a fine spray of white! And the smear of white across her cheek made her resemble an overgrown toddler at playgroup.

Her hair would have to wait, she decided as she scrubbed at her cheek . . . and her shoe would never be the same again. Ah, well!

Rhys was still grinning when she returned to the kitchen.

'You missed some!' he said, stepping away from the sink where he was washing out his paint roller. He picked up a wet cloth and advanced towards her with it. 'Here, let me!'

Before Jasmine could protest, he had taken hold of her chin, tilted her face up towards him and began to rub the cloth gently on her forehead.

'Oh!' Jasmine couldn't help the small gasp that escaped her lips.

'There! That's better!' Rhys commented, flicking the cloth away with a flourish and grinning down into her eyes.

Jasmine wondered if he was going to kiss her, and held her breath. She'd said she didn't want a romantic involvement but suddenly, she wasn't sure of that. Maybe she did?

Rhys didn't kiss her. Instead he flicked his finger at the tip of her nose.

'Coffee's ready!' he said. 'What biscuits have you got for us today?'

'Oh . . . er . . . b-butter shortbreads,' she stammered, stepping away. 'I'm . . . I'm getting a bit more used to the range now. These are cooked more evenly than the last lot.' She felt confused. Her sudden emotional response had taken her by surprise. She busied herself getting the biscuit tin out of her cupboard, hoping Rhys hadn't noticed her reaction.

'I'll take mine upstairs,' she said quickly, as Rhys handed her a mug of coffee. 'Mustn't stop for too long!' She escaped up the stairs before Rhys could comment, furious with herself for over-reacting to a friendly gesture. This was just what she didn't want! Had she made a big mistake in agreeing to share with Rhys? She hoped not.

* * *

By the end of the week, the painting was complete. The walls had been easy after the ceilings and any problems with the gloss work were overcome by judicious wiping-off and repainting. A carpet offcut was bought and a small removal van, driven by Jasmine's dad, arrived on Saturday afternoon. Her parents, Huw and Nerys, were eager to see where she was setting up in business and seemed to approve of the shared arrangement with Rhys.

'And we're going to give you a new oven as a moving-in present,' Nerys announced as they were due to leave. 'I know you want to master that range, but a standard oven will be a good back-up.'

Jasmine waved them goodbye with a lump in her throat, overwhelmed by the amount written on the cheque her dad had pressed into her hand as they departed. 'Get a dishwasher as well,' he'd urged her. 'It'll be worth its weight in gold once you get busy!'

Jasmine was too excited to sleep that night. She was wrapped up in her own duvet in her own bed, with her clothes in place in her wardrobe, dressing table and chest of drawers. She had decided to leave her sitting room as it was for the time being. Getting her tea room completed was her next priority. A few more weeks and she'd be ready to open!

It seemed as though she had just dropped off to sleep when a loud noise jolted her awake. She lay still for a moment, wondering what the noise had been. She heard a car engine spring into life and the sound of tyres making a quick departure. She leaped out of bed and ran across the landing into her sitting room.

She opened the window and looked to the left and right — but the car had gone. Still uneasy, she padded back to her bedroom and slipped into her dressing gown and slippers. She knew she wouldn't rest easy until she was sure all was well downstairs.

She had only gone down a couple of steps when Rhys appeared at his bedroom door, tousle-haired and sleepy.

'What was the noise?' he mumbled.

'I don't know. I'm going to check downstairs.'

'Hang on a mo . . . I'll be right with you!'

Jasmine continued on her way down the stairs but was glad that Rhys was only a few steps behind her when she stepped into the empty room that was to be her tea room.

The large picture-glass window had a jagged hole in the middle.

'Don't move!' Rhys ordered as she made a move to step forward.

Jasmine froze as the overhead lights illuminated the room. Shards of broken glass littered the floor and a large brick lay in their midst, with a piece of paper fastened around it.

Jasmine picked it up with trembling hands and removed the elastic bands that held the paper in place. She gasped as she read its contents.

'GET BACK TO WHERE YOU CAME FROM! YOU AREN'T WANTED HERE!'

4

Jasmine gasped. 'Oh! Who's done this?' Shaking, she turned and thrust the paper at Rhys, who read it and frowned as he shook his head.

'I don't know. You posted the required notices and no-one complained.'

'Except for the hotel.'

'Yes, but they wouldn't do this. And, like Lona said, you won't be a direct competitor with them. They'll still get the customers who prefer a bit of class . . . no offence meant, but you know what I mean!'

'Maybe someone else was thinking about opening a tea room but I unwittingly got in first?'

Rhys shrugged. 'Maybe. Who can say? I'll ring the police, shall I? I think it's the best thing — just in case it gets taken any further.'

'Oh!' Jasmine felt shaken. 'Is that likely?'

'Depends how keen they are to make you give up. They may try again. Let's get it noted from the start.'

It was nearly four o'clock in the morning before Jasmine dejectedly made her way back to bed. The police had given her the phone number of a 24-hour glazing service who had come out and boarded up the window and, as there was nothing to identify the culprit, the policeman said she could sweep up the broken glass. They would send someone round as soon as possible.

'I'll sleep at the foot of the stairs in my sleeping bag,' Rhys promised, 'just in case the perpetrators come back.'

'You can't do that!' Jasmine objected.

'Yes, I can. I'm used to sleeping rough. It's no problem.'

Jasmine didn't sleep well and was glad when daylight streaked the sky and she was justified in getting up. A police officer called round mid-morning but, when he had examined the scene and the brick and taken fingerprints from the hand-written message, he only reiterated what his night-duty colleague had said. There was nothing to identify the culprit. The only fingerprints on the paper were those of Jasmine and Rhys.

'Keep alert to anyone taking an undue interest in your property,' he advised, 'and let us know if you have any further problems.'

Jasmine decided to have morning coffee at the local hotel and, once there, asked to speak to the manager. He seemed perfectly genuine in his dismay at what had happened and assured her that their objections had been no more than a token gesture.

'We'll probably gain as much as we might lose from day visitors staying in the village for a longer period,' he said. 'There's no way anyone from here has resorted to such an action.'

Jasmine believed him. It had been a far-fetched idea anyway — because, sitting uncomfortably at the back of her mind, was the niggling suspicion that the perpetrator was none other than her ex-boyfriend, Carl. But would he go as far as that? She didn't think so . . . but a niggling doubt remained.

She telephoned Darys later when she knew she would be off-duty.

'You've not told Carl where my tea room is, have you?' she asked, after telling her what had happened and mentioning her suspicions.

'No way! What d'you think I am?' Darys retorted. 'I don't even give him the time of day!'

'What about anyone else?'

'We — ell, some of the girls know — but they all know you don't want Carl pestering you. No one's going to shop your whereabouts to him!'

'I hope not. You will remind them, won't you? It's all going so well here. I can't wait for you to come down and see how much progress we've made!'

'We?' Darys queried, a gurgle of laughter in her voice. 'What sort of progress are you talking about, eh? You and that hunky Rhys Morgan?'

'No!' Jasmine laughed. 'I've told you, I'm playing it cool with Rhys. I thought Carl was hunky at first! Once bitten, twice shy.'

'Yeah, but don't be too shy! There's a whole lot of girls out there waiting to give you a run for your money — and a few here that I'm holding in check!'

'I'll have to take that chance. Do what you can to keep Carl off my back.'

'Will do. See you, babe.'

So, having only a bunch of suspicions but no proof, she kept her counsel on that score when Rhys asked if she had any thoughts about who might be targeting her and professed to have no further culprits in mind.

With so much work still to do, Jasmine put the matter resolutely behind her and concentrated on the work in hand.

She was beginning to feel that her whole life revolved around climbing up and down the stepladder, but she was becoming more proficient and more confident in her skills. She wanted the walls to be ready for the local joiner arriving to install her refrigerated food store and display cabinet. He was going to construct it to form a quarter-oval shape around the doorway that led from the kitchen. That door was to be changed for a professional-kitchen swinging door to enable her to have plates in both hands when passing in either direction, and the counter top was to have a hinged section and a smaller swinging door to avoid any delay in serving food and drinks to customers seated in the tea room. A self-service cool drinks cabinet was on order, due to arrive within the next ten days. She wanted everything up and running for the Whitsuntide weekend — her planned opening.

Rhys was just as busy getting his gallery ready. He worked much faster than Jasmine and, since she had refused his offer to help her finish painting the tea room walls, he ordered the wood he needed and set about constructing the display shelves he had designed. He also framed a number of his paintings, which he then set about hanging on the walls.

'Have you got a minute?' he asked Jasmine part way through one afternoon about a week later.

'Sure,' she readily agreed. 'Just let me finish this bit of skirting board and it will be an ideal time to take a break.'

'It's looking great,' Rhys complimented her, glancing around. His eyes narrowed speculatively as he glanced around. 'What are you going to display on your walls?'

Ah! She'd wondered if he would get around to that.

'I've not decided yet,' she answered airily, mentally crossing her fingers as she made the last few dabs with her paintbrush. 'Any ideas?'

'A few paintings wouldn't go amiss . . . carefully selected local scenes.'

Jasmine straightened up and put the lid firmly on the paint can. 'Hmm! Any particular ones in mind?'

'You know darn well I have!' he grinned. 'How about it? I'd give you a small commission on any you sold.'

'How about a reciprocal gesture?'

'Such as?'

'What are you planning to have on your frontage?'

'Apart from my van, you mean?'

'You can park round the back. That's where my car will be, once I open.'

'I'd thought of displaying a painting on a easel, padlocked to the wall, of course — just to let people know that I'm here.'

'That won't take up much room. How about letting me have a few tables out there?'

'Wouldn't they block the view of my display window?'

'A little, I suppose . . . but you'll have a sign above your window, won't you? Have you designed it yet?'

'A few. Come and see.'

Jasmine stuck her paintbrush in a jar of thinners and followed Rhys through the door into his gallery.

'Very nice!' she enthused. 'I like your shelves.'

He had chosen light pinewood, and scattered around were lengths of genuine driftwood that he obviously intended to use as part of his decor.

'I might get some netting and a few large shells and glass floats . . . play up the seaside theme. What d'you think?'

'Fine. So, where are these signs? Have you settled on a name yet?'

'I just thought 'The Gallery'. Keep it simple,' he shrugged, showing her a few designs he had sketched. 'What about you?'

Jasmine was considering which of his signs she liked best, trying to imagine the front aspect of the two properties. 'Well, I was thinking of 'Jasmine's'. It's simple. People would find it easy to remember. But . . . '

She paused, wondering how he would take her next suggestion. 'What if I call it 'The Gallery Tea Shop'? I know we are two separate businesses but, if they seem to belong together, visitors will see your gallery advertised twice and my tables won't seem out of place.'

He gave her an admiring grin. 'You'd already thought it out, hadn't you?'

'A little.' She grinned back with a slight shrug. 'And I'm sure it would work out okay. Especially since we've left the connecting door in situ so that the customers can pass from your place to mine or vice versa. It could boost both our businesses.'

Rhys held out his hand. 'It's a deal!'

Jasmine felt her cheeks warming as Rhys took her hand in his. His eyes held a depth of emotion that made her heart beat faster and she felt herself swaying towards him, her lips slightly parted.

For a few fleeting seconds, their lips touched and it was as if a shaft of fire was burning through her. Jasmine was so startled, she pulled away. Her wide-eyed gaze seemed frozen on her face. Rhys's bemused smile made her feel like a silly schoolgirl reacting to a first kiss. In one sense, she was. Carl's kisses had never felt like that. Nor had anyone else's.

'I — I'll put the kettle on,' she stammered. 'My chocolate cake should just be about cooled. We'll seal our deal with that.'

She fled to her kitchen, her cheeks flaming with embarrassment at her gauche response. *Cup of tea and chocolate cake, indeed! Caviar and champagne would have been more appropriate. Take a few deep breaths, girl. Calm down.*

She flung open the fridge and grabbed a pot of double cream to serve with a wedge of the dark, gooey cake. Phew! The cool air felt good as it flowed towards her.

By the time Rhys came into the kitchen, she was fully prepared. With the width of the kitchen table between them, she forked up a portion of chocolate cake dripping with cream.

'To your gallery and my tea shop!' she toasted.

'The Gallery Tea Shop!'

* * *

Late in the evening, Rhys was shuffling some papers together when he spotted the pencilled sketch he had begun of Jasmine the day they met. He drew it out of the pile and nodded appraisingly. He'd caught her likeness quite well. He picked up a pencil and added a few strokes, smiling with satisfaction at the improvement. He hoped she would like it — but her reaction often caught him by surprise. An extremely independent young woman, indeed. He was learning not to push himself too far forward with her, but had nearly slipped up that afternoon. He smiled as he remembered the brief touch of her lips. If she hadn't stepped away quite so smartly that might have opened things up between them — or made things awkward. He wasn't sure which. Still, they had plenty of time for something more than friendship to develop.

He put the sketch back on the cupboard top, deciding to show it to her tomorrow. With a satisfied glance around his almost-ready gallery, he switched off the light. Mmm! Life was promising to be good!

* * *

Jasmine was down to breakfast before him the next day. He remembered that she was going to choose her floor covering this morning and needed to be back before lunchtime because the new large window was being fitted that afternoon.

'Good morning!' he greeted her breezily.

'Oh! Yes, er, good morning,' she replied somewhat hesitantly.

Rhys thought she looked far from pleased to see him, a feeling intensified when she added quietly, 'I've made you a bacon sandwich.'

'Oh, thanks. I'll make some coffee, shall I?'

'No, thank you. I've had mine. I'm just on my way out.'

She was avoiding meeting his eyes and Rhys sensed she was upset about something. Before he could ask if anything was the matter, she continued, 'There are some letters for you. I've put them on the counter in your gallery. I'll be back around lunchtime, okay?'

And, with that, she was gone.

Rhys frowned. She had seemed all right last evening. Neither had referred to their brief kiss; nor had either of them made any move to be anything more than friendly; but the atmosphere had been pleasant. He had had no cause to think that she resented their brief moment of intimacy. He poured water onto his coffee. So, what had upset her?

Feeling a little perturbed by the rift in their easy relationship, he carried his sandwich and mug through to the gallery and glanced at his mail. Nothing exciting, just a couple of catalogues he'd sent for. As he tossed them back onto the counter, he frowned and picked them up again. Where was his sketch of Jasmine? He was sure he'd left it there on the counter last night.

Had Jasmine seen it and taken it with her? Somehow, he didn't think so. She wouldn't assume it was for her, though he intended to give it to her eventually, after he had used it as a basis for a portrait in oils. No, it must have slipped on to the floor.

He glanced around but it wasn't there. Wait a minute! He bent down and took a crumpled piece of paper out of the wastepaper basket. Disbelievingly, he smoothed it out on the countertop and stared at the spoiled image. Why had she done that? It couldn't have been that she didn't like the drawing. It was a good likeness, and caught her fresh beauty. It was a sketch anyone would have been pleased to have had drawn of them.

No — it must be that she didn't want him to have drawn her! Was she sending him the message to back off? Disappointingly, it certainly seemed so. He felt like screwing the sketch back into a ball and tossing it back into the wastepaper bin but something stopped him. He knew she wasn't keen to rush headlong into a romantic interlude with him, but he'd felt they were becoming friends. Something must have happened in a past relationship to make her as wary as she was of becoming too close to anyone.

The question was, did he want to be the one to help her to leave the past behind and look to the future? Or, was Jasmine making it abundantly clear to him that he wasn't the one for her?

5

Jasmine was thankful that she had already made it known that she was to rush off early that morning, and she was doubly thankful to have been able to do so within minutes of Rhys coming down for breakfast. She knew she hadn't exactly been bright and cheery during those few minutes but considering how hurt she felt, she didn't think she had done too badly.

She wished she hadn't let her curiosity get the better of her but, when she saw the crumpled piece of drawing paper in Rhys's wastepaper bin, she had wondered what sort of sketch he had thought fit to throw away. What were his early sketches like? Did he doodle? Or did he draw to exact specifications from the outset of a work? With an attraction growing between them, she wanted to know. In fact, her sleeping thoughts had been of him and she had awoken with a sense of budding excitement as to what might become of their tentative moves towards each other.

All of that had been shattered when she had smoothed out the paper and seen that he had crushed and tossed away a very good likeness of herself. It couldn't have been because it didn't reach some absurdly high standard of perfection . . . because, to her untutored eye, it was a very accomplished sketch. Especially since he must have done it from memory, as she had never noticed him drawing her in her presence.

No, he must have drawn it in the early days of their time together and, only yesterday, decided that he no longer wanted it. And she didn't have to search far to find a reason. She had rejected his advances when he tried to kiss her yesterday afternoon, and he had now written her off.

Well, if that was the way he wanted it,

fine by her! Wasn't that just what she had told him at the outset, and had been telling herself every day since?

So why was she feeling so upset about it? She should be glad that he felt the same way — and that there would now be no danger of her forgetting her resolution to give romance a wide berth for the foreseeable future. The problem was, she didn't feel happy about it at all.

Two hours later, her choice of floor covering selected, paid for and delivery date agreed, Jasmine headed back into Manorbier. She meant to park her car at the rear of the property, in the narrow lane that gave access to their small rear yard and garden but, as she approached the front of their premises, she froze in complete stupefaction, her feet automatically stamping down on the clutch and brake pedals, both hands tightening on the wheel. A huge pile of rotting manure had been dumped on the forecourt!

Jasmine stared at it. What on earth

was that doing there? Who had ordered it?

The toot of a horn behind her jerked her out of her daze. She took her foot off the clutch pedal and promptly stalled the car. Bother!

The driver tooted again and she made an agitated twist at her ignition key. At her third attempt, the engine burst into life and she pulled carefully across the road and edged against the kerb just in front of the offending pile. Yanking on the handbrake, she released her safety belt and leaped out of her car, trying to step carefully around the huge mound.

Rhys was standing unsmiling, the backs of his hands against his hips.

'Rhys! Whatever is that . . . ?'

'Back in time to admire the effect!' Rhys said, with an eyebrow raised quizzically, ignoring her half-spoken question. 'Well, this is a message loud and clear!'

Jasmine halted. 'What's that supposed to mean?'

‘You tell me! Isn’t this what they call in the vernacular ‘a load of . . . ’!’

His lips snapped closed on the last word but Jasmine was in no doubt what the word was intended to be. She felt a warm flush burst across her cheeks. How dare he?

‘You should know!’ she cast back, thinking of her crushed face in the waste bin. ‘I expect someone from your past has caught up with you!’

‘There’s nothing in my past to warrant this!’ he snapped. ‘I was thinking of someone much closer to home!’

Jasmine’s mouth dropped open. ‘Me? You think *I’ve* done this?’

‘Well, haven’t you?’

‘Of course not! I might have been upset earlier but I wasn’t that upset!’

‘So, how upset were you?’

Jasmine hesitated. She hadn’t meant to admit to feeling upset about the sketch Rhys had thrown away. She forced a disdainful look onto her face and shrugged her shoulders. ‘Not upset at all, if you really want to know. Now, are you going to arrange for its removal? Or shall we decide to open a garden centre instead?'

With her nose very firmly in an elevated position, she picked her way around the pile of manure and marched into the tea shop. How dare he think she would stoop so low as to do a thing like that! Why, it had never even occurred to her to suppose Rhys had ordered it! But she certainly hadn't.

She threw her car keys onto the table and crossed the kitchen to pick up the kettle, feeling in great need of the British panacea for all ills.

Then, who has? a little voice asked deep within. *Carl?* She hoped not.

She realised Rhys had followed her inside and was leaning against the doorjamb with his arms folded across his chest.

'So, if it wasn't you, who was it?' he asked.

'How should I know? Didn't you ask the man who delivered it? Why didn't you stop him dumping it?'

'I was painting in my studio. I didn't hear him ring the bell. The first I knew was the sound of the engine tipping up the back of his trailer. I tried to attract his attention by banging on the window but he didn't hear. By the time I got downstairs, it was too late.'

'Didn't you tell him it was a mistake, and make him load it up again?'

'What do you think? That I said, 'Thank you very much,' and gave him a tip for the delivery?'

Jasmine felt her cheeks flush. 'No . . . but it's still there!'

Rhys shrugged himself away from the doorjamb.

'He said he'd need orders from his boss and to get a time re-assigned.'

'Oh.' There wasn't much else to say. 'D'you want a cup of tea?'

'Yes, please, since you're making one.'

He moved forward and stood looking down at her.

'So, who's got a grudge against you?

Who would go out of his or her way to do something like this?'

'Her?' Jasmine queried. She hadn't considered it being a woman. Still, that let Carl off the hook, didn't it? Unless he had got someone else to make the phone call? Would he really be prepared to go that far? He could easily have persuaded someone to make the call. He'd say it was a joke or some such pretext.

But what should she do? If she phoned and challenged him, he'd only deny it and probably then use the occasion to try to get back together with her. And she had no proof, only a niggling suspicion.

'I telephoned the garden centre and the manager said a woman had phoned in the order, with specific instructions to dump it at the front,' she realised Rhys was saying. 'She said there was no access at the rear and that we'd wheel it through ourselves.'

Jasmine shrugged. 'Look, I really don't know who's done it. And, anyway, if it was a woman who ordered the delivery, what makes you so sure it was directed against me? It could be someone with a grudge against you. Who have you upset lately?'

'No one that I know of, except you.' He grinned lopsidedly. 'Mr Nice Guy, that's me. Hadn't you noticed?'

'Huh!' She pushed a mug of tea towards him. 'So, do you at least accept it wasn't me?'

She raised her eyes and looked expectantly at his face. His expression held reservations, but at least it was no longer directing anger at her.

'You have said it wasn't, and I believe you, but I'm not totally convinced you have no suspicions about who the culprit might be.'

Jasmine tried to hold his gaze but it was she who looked away first. What could she say? Should she be honest with him, even though she wasn't sure? After a brief hesitation, she said, 'My last boyfriend didn't want us to split up — but I can't really believe he'd do anything like this.'

'And the broken window, too? Could that have been him?'

Jasmine shrugged. 'I don't know. I haven't told him where I've moved to, but I suppose he could have found out if he was determined enough. I felt I was being followed once or twice before I began sleeping here. Oh, I don't know. In one sense, it would be easier to cope with if it is him — because, if it's not, I haven't a clue who it is!'

She looked so woebegone that Rhys put down his mug of tea and wrapped his arms around her.

'Cheer up. We'll be on the alert from now on — and maybe you could get word back to him that we've got the police involved. That should act as some sort of deterrent, shouldn't it?'

Before Jasmine could imagine there was anything more than a brotherly sort of affection behind the hug, Rhys dropped his arms and stepped away. He felt they had arrived at the correct conclusion and doubted any more would come of it. Being openly honest in his own dealings with the opposite sex, he found it hard to imagine anyone being so jealous or prepared to do devious acts to try to hold on to someone's affections, but it did go somewhere along the line to explain Jasmine's reservations about leaping into a new relationship too readily. He wished he could convince her that it wouldn't be like that if she opened up towards him, but he knew that only time, not persuasive words, would heal any residual hurts she had sustained — and time was something they surely had plenty of!

* * *

The manure was carted away two days later and a heavy downpour of rain removed most of the tell-tale signs left behind. When Jasmine later ordered new paving flags from the same garden centre and hired the staff to lay them, the manager gave a discount on the price as a sign of goodwill, thus offsetting part of the cost of the unpleasant hoax.

With the outer trappings of a harmonious relationship restored between herself and Rhys, Jasmine was happy to push on with the work to transform the former village store into a modern tea shop. The new floor tiles were laid and the joiner came to construct the fittings and install the new appliances. Everything was beginning to take shape, and seemed to be on target for opening at Whitsuntide.

Rhys had completed all the renovations he needed to do, and was concentrating on traversing the local countryside and coastal path to make sketches of places of local interest. The mediaeval castle featured in a number of proposed paintings, along with countless spectacular coves surrounded by high rugged cliffs, many inhabited by the wheeling and shrieking sea birds. He found beautiful bays such as

Barafundle Bay, Broadhaven and Swanlake Bay; and inland delights such as Bosherton Lily Ponds, which would be even more breathtaking, he was promised, at the beginning of July when the lilies were in bloom. And slightly inland was the beautiful village intriguingly called Stepaside which he found one day when driving to Wiseman's Bridge to investigate some former mining tunnels that had been cut through the headland and led to the harbour at Saundersfoot. It would take a lifetime to capture even a part of Nature's bountiful treasures in this area!

Jasmine had accompanied him on some of his wanderings and they enjoyed a friendly camaraderie that proved how similar many of their views and tastes were. Yet although Rhys sometimes seemed as though he might like to take their relationship a step further, mindful of her spoken desire to establish her new business before embarking on a romantic friendship, he always pulled back.

At first, Jasmine was glad that he did. She couldn't rid herself of the memory of the trapped feeling she had known as her relationship with Carl had developed, nor of the uncertainty of who had thrown the brick through her window and arranged for the manure to be dumped on their forecourt. She didn't seriously suspect Rhys, but the knowledge that he'd suspected her gave her no confidence that a closer relationship between them might work. No, it was far better to keep things as they were!

Perversely, there were times when she wished they were closer . . . and then she berated herself for her lack of resolution and feminine weakness. She liked him well enough, but she didn't want anything to get in the way of her burgeoning business.

A few early tourists noticed the developing tea room and called in on the off-chance for a hot drink and a snack. Jasmine knew she couldn't sell them anything she had prepared on the premises, as she hadn't yet had her premises passed by the public health inspectors, but she saw no harm in offering them a friendly cup of tea or coffee free of charge and inviting them to buy from a selection of pre-packed biscuits and cakes she'd bought from the wholesale warehouse. Since everyone promised to return later in the year and to pass on the word, Jasmine considered the cost as part of her advertising budget and building up a future clientele. And, once her chilled drinks cabinet was up and running, she sold canned and bottled drinks as well, delighting in the sound of the till as each transaction was completed.

Rhys sold a number of paintings and took specific commissions for others, and was confident that the coming season would launch him as a popular local artist.

The first inspection of the tea room took place just after Easter. Work was still in progress, but the inspector poked about in corners, took swabs of work surfaces and listened to Jasmine's projected plan of operations. He gave her a detailed list of required practices and asked her to let him know when she was ready to undergo the next, hopefully, qualifying, inspection.

She was ready three weeks later. Her outdoor tables hadn't yet arrived but that was no drawback. The area was prepared and had no safety hazards. The inspector had asked her to prepare a limited amount of samples of what she intended to sell to the public and to set out the tea room as if she were open for business. The day before the proposed inspection, Jasmine cleaned and baked in a frenzy of activity, and it was Rhys who finally called her to a halt.

'It couldn't be any more hygienic if a whole army of cleaners had been in here,' he assured her, 'and I've survived your cooking for the past couple of months. Everything will pass muster, believe me. Your work practices are clearly detailed; your check lists of daily prep and cleaning routines are in order; and copies of your menu are on the tables. Go and get ready for bed . . . and give me a shout when the bathroom is clear. I'll switch off the lights.'

Jasmine lay awake for a while, going over her preparations for tomorrow. The bakery would be delivering bread rolls in the morning; fresh salads and cooked meats were coming from a local delicatessen; and her milk delivery had been increased for the day. Potatoes were scrubbed in readiness for baking and a selection of prepared dishes were in the freezer.

She had done all she could.

* * *

The following day dawned sunny. A good omen, she hoped. She leaped out of bed and ran down to the bathroom, calling to Rhys as she headed back upstairs. 'Bathroom's free! I'll get the oven on for the croissants.'

No cooked breakfast today, apart

from reheating the croissants — she wouldn't be able to eat it, and wanted no complications with the cooking range being used for anything other than what was on her menu.

She dressed quickly and ran downstairs again, eager to start the day. Once the inspection was over, she could make the posters declaring her tea shop to be open for business! Her mind already racing ahead, she pushed open the kitchen door, crossed over to the oven to switch it on and then took two cereal bowls out of the cupboard. As she turned to put them on the table she involuntarily screamed and the dishes dropped from her hands, smashing into pieces as they hit the tiles.

A large rat was scurrying across the kitchen floor.

6

Rhys hurtled into the kitchen dressed wearing nothing more than his pyjama bottoms. Jasmine was standing backed up against the sink unit, her eyes wide and her fingers spread across her mouth. Rhys followed her gaze and saw the rat immediately. He swiftly covered the distance between them and took hold of her shoulders.

'Go straight upstairs. Leave it to me. I'll get rid of it.'

Jasmine fled. She knew she couldn't face chasing the thing out of her kitchen. Where had it got in? And it had had all night to spread its germs around! She'd have to start cleaning all over again — and the inspector was due within a couple of hours.

Oh, no — she would have to tell him! Her premises wouldn't be passed. Her legs felt as if they were about to collapse under her and she sat down quickly on the edge of her bed. It wasn't fair! She had everything ready.

She eventually heard Rhys's footsteps coming upstairs. He knocked on her door and she called, 'Come in.'

He crossed the room and sat beside her, taking her hands in his. 'I had to kill it. I had it cornered and there was no other way to get it out.'

'What have you done with it?'

'I've put it in a bag, outside at the back.'

'I'll have to tell the inspector, won't I?'

'I'm afraid so.'

'Oh, Rhys! Why today of all days? And how did it get in? There's been no sign of mice, let alone rats! Did it come in from the garden, d'you think?'

'I don't see how. You've not had the back door open much, have you? And you only finished cleaning yesterday. Surely it couldn't have been lurking anywhere! We'll have to check all skirting boards and make sure there are no holes anywhere.'

They did that immediately. They looked in every downstairs room; pulled everything out of the cupboards, especially the kitchen units; traced every inch of skirting board; examined each outer door to make sure they fitted well, and every window. Everywhere seemed to be just as it should be.

'Could someone have pushed it through the letterbox?' Jasmine finally wondered. 'It looked huge. Was it small enough to fit through?'

Rhys shrugged. 'I wouldn't have thought so . . . but I suppose it could be possible. Mice can almost flatten themselves out. Maybe rats can do the same. Whoever pushed it through would have had to wear thick gloves. But how would it have got into the kitchen? You usually close each door at night, don't you?'

Jasmine looked at him thoughtfully. 'You were last upstairs last night. Was there no sign of it then?'

'No. And I did shut the door. I

ushered you out of here and didn't come back in. Were both doors shut when you came in here this morning?'

She thought back, re-enacting in her mind her entry into the kitchen.

'No . . . at least, not the one from the passageway into the kitchen,' she said slowly. 'The door was open. I'm sure it was.'

Her unspoken accusation hovered in the air between them. Rhys looked uncomfortable.

'I was sure I'd closed it. I'm sorry if I didn't, but I can't see that it makes much difference. How did the rat get into the house in the first place? We've not seen any trace of one.'

They sat silently for a moment or two, each with their own thoughts. It was Rhys who eventually broke the silence.

'Let's get some breakfast. I'll put the croissants in, shall I?' he suggested. 'Then we'll start cleaning everywhere. You never know. If everywhere is scrupulously clean, the inspector might still sign the authorisation to start serving food.'

They weren't given that chance. There was a ring at the front door before they had had time to eat their bowls of cereal. Jasmine went through the tea room to see who it was, hoping it might be the postman with something too big to fit through the letterbox, but it wasn't. She recognised the inspector from his previous visit. With a sinking heart she unlocked the door and stood aside to allow him into the tea room.

'Sorry to come earlier than expected,' he apologised, 'but we had a phone call. A report that rats had been found on your premises and that there was a possibility that you might try to get rid of the evidence.'

Jasmine stared at him.

'A phone call! Who was it? Did they leave a name or contact number?'

'I'm afraid I couldn't say. It would be confidential information, in any case. Is the report true?'

Jasmine made a rueful grimace.

'The first part is — though it was 'rat' in the singular. But we weren't intending to conceal the fact. You'd better come in and see for yourself.'

The inspector listened to all she had to say, poked about in cupboards and searched for possible entrance holes but, like Jasmine and Rhys earlier, found no satisfactory explanation. He stroked his chin thoughtfully.

'It's not unusual for us to receive anonymous phone calls about such matters but, in this case, I'd go as far as to say that it is unusual in so far as it is on this specific day and there has been no previous incident. Whoever made the call had to know about this particular rat being on the premises today. Who knew I was due to call today?'

Jasmine spread her hands helplessly. 'My parents knew; as did a few of my friends from where I used to work. Oh, and the lady who owns the premises — but none of them would do anything like this! And, anyway, we still have the problem of how anyone managed to get the rat into the house. All the outside doors were locked.'

'Is there anyone who would profit by you being denied a licence?'

'Not really . . . not that I know of . . . though there have been a couple of other incidents.' She quickly described them. 'But I don't see how anyone could have done this!'

Not even Carl. Her thoughts strayed to her friend Darys. She knew Darys wouldn't have told Carl about the inspection, but had anyone else passed the word on to him? If he really wanted to know, he would be like a ferret with a rabbit in its sights. So it was possible that he knew where she was, she supposed. But even he would still have had the problem of getting the rat into the kitchen. She shook her head.

'I just don't know.'

'And all doors were locked this morning when you came downstairs?'

'Yes. That is . . . I didn't try the back door.' She looked at Rhys, remembering his slip-up in not closing the inner door. 'You took the rat out that way, didn't you, Rhys? Was the door locked?'

'Yes. I had to unlock it to get out with it . . . and you've just unlocked the front door to let the inspector in. So both doors were locked.'

'Were the doors bolted, as well?' the inspector asked.

'No — at least, not the back door. It has a bolt, but it doesn't line up with the bolt-hole, so we can't use it.'

'Even so, unless some unauthorised person has a key, there still doesn't seem to be a reasonable explanation,' the inspector mused. 'I'd check up on that, if I were you, and get the bolt fixed as an added precaution. Now, I can't pass your premises today, Miss Jones, but, because of the circumstances involved, I'll come back a week from today and do the inspection then. Good day to you both.'

With the inspector gone, Jasmine returned to the kitchen. The smell of overdone croissants filled the air and Rhys was scraping their charred remains off the baking tray into the waste bin. Jasmine sat disconsolately at the table. She pushed the bowl of soggy cornflakes aside. Her thoughts were a confused jumble. Uncomfortably, she found herself with Carl at the top of her list of suspects — but how could he have done it? Had the rat been there longer than they supposed? It would have to have been drugged into a stupor and cunningly concealed somewhere! But how likely was that? With both outer doors securely locked, it pointed to an inside job, and that meant Rhys! She flicked her eyes across to where he was leaning against the sink unit and was startled to find that he was watching her intently.

He cocked his eyebrow questioningly. 'What are you thinking?'

'I . . . I don't know,' she stammered, unwilling to voice her thoughts.

Rhys pushed himself upright and came towards her. His expression was ruefully tender as he touched her shoulder.

'It wasn't me, Jasmine.'

Jasmine sighed. 'If you say so,' she agreed, though with enough doubt in her voice to make the words meaningless.

Rhys went into his gallery, leaving Jasmine seated by the table. He supposed he could understand why she suspected that he could be responsible for the acts against her; — but he was disappointed that she had such little faith in him.

One thing he could do was to fix the bolt socket. It only needed adjusting a little. He should have done it weeks ago, but it hadn't seemed a priority.

He did that, and then, since it was raining and he didn't expect any customers, went up to his studio to paint. After a few abortive efforts, he irritably cleaned his brushes, picked up a lightweight waterproof jacket and went back downstairs.

'I'm going to Tenby for some art materials,' he told Jasmine. 'Can I get you anything?'

'No, thanks.' Thinking that sounded a

bit cool, she added, 'Have a coffee before you go — and a cookie. They're oat and walnut, a new recipe.'

Taking it as the olive branch it was intended to be, Rhys agreed, but conversation was a little stilted between them and, after ten minutes or so, he stood up and took his mug to the sink to rinse it.

'I'll be off, then. See you later.' He paused in the doorway. 'Er, I might go to Camarthen and see if any of my old mates are free this evening, so don't cook anything for me. Oh, and don't lock me out, will you?' He raised his eyebrow and was relieved to see a spark of merriment in Jasmine's eyes.

'I might!' she threatened. 'It depends how late you are!'

Rhys felt his mood lighten as he drove along the country lanes towards Tenby, though he frowned a little as he turned on to the main road about five minutes later. He hadn't been entirely truthful as to his intended destination. Tenby was merely a town en route . . .

because it wasn't his old mates he was hoping to meet up with, but Jasmine's. And he had better be discreet because he knew that Jasmine would be justifiably angry if she found out!

* * *

Jasmine felt miserable after Rhys had gone. She knew she hadn't exactly hidden her suspicions of his possible involvement, but she had tried to make amends by offering him the coffee and cookies. Surely he must understand her predicament? After all, what did they really know about each other? Not all that much, she conceded.

Not that she really believed Rhys was up to some underhand game. Surely her judgment of character wasn't that poor? Though, considering her initial misplaced trust in Carl, possibly it was.

She paced around the kitchen, unable to settle to anything constructive. This was to have been a red-letter day in her plans for the tea shop — the official go-ahead to settle on an opening date. Instead, she felt thoroughly deflated. And Rhys had said he would help her to clean — but what had he done but blithely desert her! She supposed she ought to buckle down to it herself, but she couldn't summon the enthusiasm to begin.

The phone rang. It was her mother. 'How did the inspection go, dear?'

'Oh, Mum!'

Jasmine couldn't help it. Her voice broke as she poured out her desolation at the morning's events. She hesitated to voice her suspicions about Carl. Her mum had never taken to him and was quite likely to say, 'I told you he was no good.' Instead, she spoke of her perplexity and intention to spend the day scrubbing every square inch of any surface the rat could have touched.

'If it can be left until tomorrow, I'll drive over and help you,' Nerys Jones offered. 'Your father can manage without me for once.'

'Oh, thanks, Mum.'

They chatted a little more and then bade each other farewell until the following day. Jasmine felt better already. Now, what was she to do for the rest of today? She looked at all the things that had been hauled out of the cupboards. They could wait until tomorrow when her mother was here. If she moved them aside a little, she could continue with her baking — but, somehow that didn't appeal. No, what she wanted was a bit comfort and consolation! And she knew the very person to give it to her. She would drive over to Cardigan and get in touch with Darys.

She rang Darys' mobile, but guessed from the non-response that it was turned off. That probably meant she was at work. That was good. If she was at work now, she would more than likely be off after two o'clock.

Revising her plan to leave immediately, she made a sandwich for later and then had a shower, washing away her despondency from the aborted Health and Safety inspection. She grinned wryly at her reflection in the mirror when she caught herself singing, 'I'm gonna wash that rat right out of my hair!' Heavens! Where was her street cred? Anyone who didn't know the hotel staff had performed excerpts from *South Pacific* last Christmas would wonder if they had had a timeslip back into the middle of the last century!

By the time she was on her way to Cardigan, the rain had stopped and weak rays of sunshine were penetrating through the clouds. Jasmine felt her usual lightheartedness reasserting itself and she realised that, far from meeting Darys to weep on her shoulder, she was actually looking forward to seeing her friend again for a girlish natter. No doubt Darys would want to know how things were progressing between her and Rhys, but she would manage to parry any awkward questions and keep Darys guessing.

When she saw by the clock on the dashboard that it was 2.15p.m., she pulled over and tried Darys' mobile again. Still no response. She must still have it switched off. Never mind! With any luck she would be back at the flat by now. However, it wasn't Darys who answered when she phoned.

'I'm sorry. You've just missed her,' the young woman's voice said regretfully. 'This gorgeous man came to the hotel for her and she just dashed in to change into something more glamorous! They've gone for a late lunch somewhere. I'm not sure where. Can I take a message for her?'

'That's okay. I'll surprise her! I think I know where they'll have gone.'

Jasmine grinned gleefully. So, Darys had a new man in her life and hadn't told her! And they used to share everything! Well, not *quite* all . . . but usually the uncertain beginnings of a new romance . . .

Jasmine parked her car and headed confidently to their favourite rendezvous. It was popular with couples wanting to get to know each other as it had pleasant alcoves with delicate fretwork and lacy plants subdividing many of the tables. With any luck, either Bruno or Cesare, two of the waiters she knew, would be on duty and able to point her in the right direction.

As it happened, she didn't need any friendly waiter to assist her to find Darys and her new man. Jasmine spotted them from across the road just as they were about turn into the restaurant. Her hand had half-risen to attract their attention but the gleeful smile died on her face.

The man whose face was smiling down at her friend should have been miles away in Tenby or Camarthen — for it was none other than Rhys Morgan!

7

Jasmine felt her face stiffen in disbelief. For a moment or two, her mind refused to function and she just stared across the road as the oblivious couple ran laughing up the steps and disappeared through the doorway. It was only when Jasmine became aware that passers-by were looking at her strangely that she forced herself to step away from the edge of the kerb and move back to the more anonymous background of the shop fronts.

Rhys and Darys? She didn't know they were seeing each other. Had their friendship begun when Darys visited her? Surely she would have noticed. And what about the tender looks he'd been giving her? What was his game?

Jasmine felt her legs begin to shake and tried to pull herself together. She had no rights of ownership over Rhys. If he wanted to take out a girl — any girl — he had every right to do so. But why Darys? And why hadn't he said?

More importantly — why hadn't Darys thought to mention anything to her?

She knew she ought to cross the road and follow her two friends inside and exclaim at how incredible it was that they were seeing each other. When reading romantic novels and the heroine had run away from such a confrontation, she had always snorted in disbelief, thinking, *Get in there, girl! Sort it out!* But she couldn't.

Well, one thing was for sure. She was thankful she had kept her growing feelings hidden from Rhys — *and* from Darys. When the time came to confront them, or be confronted by them, hopefully, she would have managed to compose herself and resign herself to the fact that there was no future between her and Rhys.

She hurried back to her car and set off on the return journey to Manorbier, partly glad that the brief show of sunshine had faded and dark clouds covered the sky again. They matched her mood.

It was only when she was once more on the minor road that looped its way through Manorbier that another thought struck her so forcibly that, after a hasty glance in her mirror to make sure no-one was close behind her, she indicated and pulled over partly onto the grassy verge.

What if Rhys and Darys had intentionally kept their friendship from her? What if Rhys was, after all, the perpetrator of the events that had occurred? He was the one on the spot, wasn't he? He could have done them all! But why? Did he want Darys to take over the tea room, if and when Jasmine failed or was too discouraged to continue? Is that what Darys wanted, too?

She shook her head in bewilderment. She must be mistaken. Too much devious planning would have been necessary in order to have carried it off. And neither Rhys nor Darys were capable of such deception . . . were they?

* * *

It was the following morning before Jasmine came face-to-face with Rhys. She had spent a miserable evening watching her small television and finally decided to have an early night, in the hope that, wakening refreshed after a good sleep, she would have a better chance of accepting whatever Rhys might choose to tell her.

As it was, he told her nothing.

He breezed into the kitchen with a cheery, 'Good morning!' and proceeded to ask how she'd got on with the cleaning the previous day.

'I didn't do it. Mum rang and said she would come along today to help me, so I . . . did nothing in particular.'

'Good. So, anything I can help you with today?'

'No, thanks. As I said, Mum is coming over. How did you get on?' Would he tell her about seeing Darys? 'Did you meet up with any of your mates?'

His eyes didn't quite meet hers as he replied, 'One or two. We had a few pints and I asked them to pass the word around about the gallery . . . and about your tea shop soon being ready to open. They said they'll drop by some time. You'll probably do better out of them than I will. I can't see many of them buying any of my paintings!'

Porky pies! thought Jasmine, though he could have met up with his pals later, she conceded. So, he and Darys were to remain a secret, were they?

'Oh, and I called in to see Lona when I was passing through Tenby,' Rhys added casually.

That surprised her. Either he was embellishing his deception, or he had done so after leaving Darys in Cardigan. Curiosity overcame her sceptism.

'Oh! Is she settled in her new

apartment? We've been so busy I haven't had chance to go to visit her.'

'Yes, she's fine. She said to tell you you're welcome to go any time. What I really went for though was to ask her if it's possible that any other keys to this place might be in circulation — you know, like someone who might have held a key for her in case she got locked out or anything.'

'Oh, I hadn't thought of that! And are there?'

'No. She said only she and her son ever had any and she got her son's back from him before our contracts were signed.'

'Right! Did you ask if she had ever had a problem with rats?'

'Yes. She said not in the past ten years or so. They had had a problem when the back lane was made for people to have rear access to their properties. People had longer gardens, some of them with sheds. The redevelopment disturbed the nesting grounds and made the rats look elsewhere, but the council dealt with it and there's certainly been no problem since then.'

'Good! Well, let's hope we, too, have seen the last of them!'

She still felt aggrieved by him choosing not to speak of the part of his day spent with Darys, so she hurriedly said, 'Well, thanks for going to see Lona on my behalf. I should have thought of it myself. Now, hurry up with your breakfast and then make yourself scarce so that I can be ready to start cleaning when Mum comes!'

Looking slightly surprised by her dismissal, Rhys did as he was told.

Jasmine didn't see him for the rest of the day. Nerys arrived soon after half-past nine and mother and daughter worked harmoniously side by side, giving the kitchen and the tea room a thorough going-over.

'There! As bright as a new pin!' Nerys said with some satisfaction when the job was done and she put the kettle on to boil for the umpteenth time that day. 'Where is that nice young man,

Rhys, today? Just like all men, keeping out of the way when cleaning has to be done?'

'I think he's gone out to do some painting. He has to get as much painting as he can done now, so that he'll have plenty of stock when the season starts properly in a few weeks' time.'

'Yes, of course. And how are things between you? Is sharing the premises working out all right?'

'Yes. We don't see a lot of each other; we've been too busy. It's just a business sharing of the premises, you know. Nothing personal or romantic.'

'If you say so,' Nerys agreed, clearly thinking, or hoping, it might be something more. 'Well, it's always best to start slowly and see how things develop. The same with your business. Don't try to do too much too soon.'

Jasmine was glad that her mum's thoughts were back on the tea room. 'That's exactly what I plan to do,' she agreed.

* * *

During the next few days, Jasmine concentrated on preparing and freezing such food items that she could make in advance, keeping and labelling a small sample of each batch for testing. Biscuits were packed into airtight boxes and a couple of rich fruit cakes were maturing nicely.

She was understandably nervous when the day for the inspection dawned again, but, this time, everything went off perfectly. It was a bright sunny day in early May, and the tea room sparkled. The green and white gingham tablecloths added to the clean, bright aspect and the small vases of spring flowers on each of the tables completed the picture.

The inspector, Mr Tomkins as she now knew him to be called, glanced around, nodding his head. 'It looks very nice indeed!' he commented. 'But I'll start in the kitchen. No more rats, I hope?'

'No!' Jasmine agreed hastily. 'And no other upsets either!'

'Good!' Mr Tomkins peered and poked, took swabs and sealed samples of food into plastic bags. Eventually, he turned to Jasmine with a smile.

'Everything looks fine and, as soon as I have the results of all these, I'll let you know — and, hopefully, give you the go-ahead to open to the public.' He held out his hand. 'The best of luck, my dear! I'm sure you'll do well!'

The weather was improving daily and a growing stream of customers, most of whom were on their way to or from the castle or the beach, had to be content with pre-packed snacks and bottled or canned drinks. Jasmine made time to confirm her order of tables for the outdoor area and arrange a delivery date. They were heavy-duty green plastic ones with matching chairs that could be stacked under cover at the rear of the premises when not in use. She thought the green would weather better than white and, with the same gingham cloths as inside the tea room, and plain green parasols, it made an attractive and welcoming sight.

One week after the inspection, the official letter arrived. Jasmine carried it into Rhys's gallery, where he was hanging a new painting to replace one that had been sold the day before.

'It's come!'

'Do you want me to open it?' Rhys asked, seeing her fingers trembling.

'No, I'll do it . . . but I'm scared. What if I've failed?'

'You won't have. Here! Use this.'

He handed her a letter opener. Jasmine slit open the envelope and quickly ran her eyes over the letter she drew from within.

'It's passed!' she cried. 'I can start serving real food!'

Rhys swept her into his arms and whirled her round, his face equally delighted. 'I knew it would be all right!'

As her feet touched the ground, Rhys pulled her into a firm embrace, his mouth claiming hers with a fervour that sent her senses into a whirl of ecstasy. It was minutes — or was it only seconds? she wasn't sure — before her brain detached itself from the heady aura of the kiss and, somehow, she managed to pull herself away. Her hands rested against Rhys' chest and his hands were cupped around her elbows, holding her body close to his.

'Sh . . . should we be doing this?' she whispered.

Rhys grinned. 'I don't mind, if you don't!'

That was the trouble! She didn't mind. But she should! What about Darys? Maybe Darys hadn't cared about betraying Jasmine — but she did!

'It's . . . not a good idea,' she said faintly, pushing at Rhys' chest a little more determinedly.

Her parted lips were tingling and maybe if Rhys had resisted the movement and taken her into his arms again, she would have made only a weak protest and surrendered herself once more into that wonderful bliss — but he didn't. He smiled ruefully and gave a self-deprecating shrug.

'I was so pleased for you, I forgot myself,' he apologised. 'I didn't mean anything. I tell you what!' He reached down under the counter that held his till and straightened up holding a bottle by its neck. 'Let's celebrate with this, instead. I knew everything would be okay for you, and got it in ready.'

Jasmine's eyes widened. 'Champagne?'

'Only a cheap one, but it's the real thing. And here's a couple of glasses. Let's drink to the success of our businesses, shall we?'

The tension of the previous few minutes was defused as Rhys popped the cork off the bottle and poured out the effervescent liquid. They clinked their glasses together and the sparkling bubbles leaped and danced and tickled Jasmine's nose as she sipped the champagne. It was a drink that always went straight to her head and when Rhys offered to refill her glass, she lightly waved her other hand as she set the glass down on the counter.

'Best not,' she apologised. 'I think I'll go and ring Mum and Dad — and then I'm going to put out that large notice I've had ready for days. 'Tea Room Open. 9.00 a.m. until 5.30 p.m.''

Rhys felt his mood deflate as she left him. He wished she would let him get closer to her. He tried not to think of the way her delightful curls bobbed about her face when she moved her head and how he longed to twist one of them around his finger. He grinned suddenly. Well, maybe he *would* think about it and get it out of his system.

There was a steady trickle of customers all day and Jasmine happily cooked baked potatoes with various fillings; slices of lasagne with a side salad; and spaghetti bolognaise. She'd telephoned the bakery, dairy and delicatessen to confirm her orders of bread, dairy produce and cooked meats, and managed to get a small delivery of each by mid-morning. Her own cakes and biscuits went down a treat and, by the time she was whisking off the tablecloths ready to start afresh the next day, she felt she had made — and drunk — gallons of tea and coffee. What with taking orders, cooking and serving, she was almost run off her feet and knew that she would need extra help before very long.

Rhys had made extra sales, too, as most of her customers had wandered through into the gallery after they had paid their bills.

In the evening, when all her clearing-up and preparations for the next day were completed, she decided she must telephone Darys to tell her that she was up and running, and to invite her to come over on her next day off. Enough of this pussy-footing around the subject. If Darys and Rhys had a friendship going, the sooner she started getting used to it, the better.

When Darys arrived, around mid-morning the following Tuesday, she had brought two cars full of Jasmine's ex-colleagues with her.

'They all wanted to see you in action!' Darys laughed, getting out of her car. 'Don't worry, we haven't told Carl, and no-one's going to. He's left!'

'Left?' Jasmine echoed. Any awkwardness she was anticipating on seeing her friend in possible close proximity to Rhys was instantly cast aside. 'Where's he gone?'

'Don't know, he didn't say. He had a disagreement with Mr Halston and stormed out in a huff when Mr Halston wouldn't back down.'

'Oh.' Jasmine wasn't entirely happy to hear that. She would rather know where Carl was. Now he could be anywhere! Instinctively, she looked beyond the crowd of her friends to scan the backdrop of the village street, but there was nothing untoward to see. *Get a grip, Jasmine*, she told herself. *Don't let him spoil your day!* She smiled at her friends.

'Come inside, everyone. You're just in time for morning coffee.'

Jasmine loved seeing so many of her

ex-colleagues again and revelled in their praise for her tea room venture. They were a light-hearted, almost rowdy crowd and kept Jasmine running back and forth with their orders.

'I say, waitress! There's fly in my coffee!' Jack called out as Jasmine passed his table.

'That's usually ten pence extra, sir!' Jasmine quipped back. 'But, since it's you, it's twenty!'

When a number of other visitors arrived, Darys cheerfully joined Jasmine behind the counter. 'You cook, I'll serve!' she offered. 'Oh, look, Rhys has just come in. I'll take him a coffee through, shall I? Hi, Rhys! Coffee?'

Jasmine jerked her head up and slid her gaze from Darys to Rhys, looking for signs of a special awareness of each other, but none was apparent. So, they weren't about to make their friendship known, then! The uncertainty of her thoughts seemed to strike like a knife in her stomach. Momentarily, she had forgotten; now it was back.

'Fine!' she said airily, turning away.

From then on, she felt she was acting a part, joking, smiling, flirting even with the lads who had come — but part of her attention was keeping track of where Darys and Rhys were, wondering if any of the others were aware of the possible situation. James, Darys' boyfriend, wasn't there, she noted.

Everyone else from the party wandered off, down to the shore or to look around the castle, Jasmine supposed, leaving her and Darys working together providing lunches for a number of customers.

'You're doing well! You'll need extra help soon,' Darys pointed out.

'Yes, I've placed an ad in the post office.'

'If you have no luck, I'll come and do a few days for you over the Whit holiday,' Darys offered.

'Oh!' Did she want that? Jasmine wasn't sure. She didn't have to make it *too* easy for them, did she?

'Well, er, that's . . . very kind of you!

I'll bear it in mind.'

She wasn't sure that she would — though, to be honest, she hadn't noticed Darys spending any more time talking to Rhys than any of the others had. Had she not actually seen them together in Cardigan that day, she wouldn't have suspected anything. Maybe it had been a one-off meeting for some reason, though she couldn't imagine why.

By the time lunches were over and her friends departed, accompanied by toot-tooting car horns and hands waving out of the windows, a few more visitors were drifting in for afternoon teas . . . and so it went on until closing time. What a busy day! She knew it had been boosted by her friends, but realised that many and more could turn up during the Whit holiday and, indeed, throughout the summer season. She must make sure she had employed a waitress before then,

'Wow, what a day!' Rhys spoke from the doorway to his gallery. 'It went really well, didn't it?'

Jasmine turned and smiled, pausing from piling crockery onto her tray. 'Yes. It was good to see them all again. They've swelled my coffers!'

'And mine.' He looked pleased. 'Some of them bought a number of small sketches, especially those I've made into cards. It was quite a frenzy while it lasted, wasn't it? A taste of things to come, eh?'

'I hope so.' She noticed he had a satchel containing his sketching equipment over his shoulder. 'Are you going out?'

'Yes. I want to catch the sun as it goes round the headland. I'm going up round the cliffs towards Freshwater Bay. Any chance of you coming if I help you to finish off here first?'

Jasmine's heart leaped. It would be a pleasant end to the day. Maybe whatever had been between him and Darys had fizzled out? Maybe she would find a way to ask him about it? It needed to be done. Then, she'd sit and watch Rhys sketching as she had on a few previous occasions.

She almost agreed . . . then reality restrained her. She had too much to do! When the dishwasher was loaded, she'd have to replenish her stock of cakes and cookies and prepare sandwich fillings for tomorrow. She smiled her apology.

'Sorry! I'd love to . . . but . . . ' She spread her hands around. 'Work must go on! I've sold a lot of stock today.'

'Yeah, okay. No worries. That's the price we pay in our line of business. See you later!'

It was quiet after he'd gone, in contrast to the busy day. It was something she'd have to get used to. She carried the tray through to the kitchen and began to load the dishwasher. The ding-dong of the doorbell made her straighten up. Dash! She hadn't locked the door after Rhys went out — nor had she turned the door notice to 'Closed'.

'I'm sorry. We're closed for the day,'

she said, as she stepped back into the tea room. 'Oh!'

Her heart plummeted.

The man framed in the doorway was Carl.

8

'Carl! What are you doing here?' This was one place Jasmine had hoped never to see him. How long had he known where to find her? She stood still, keeping a few tables between herself and him as he answered her question.

'What do you think? I've come to see you, of course! Did you think I'd just forget all about you?'

'No. I'm just surprised to see you. How did you know where to find me?'

'Well, certainly not because you gave me directions, like you did the rest of our crowd! They came by invitation, didn't they?'

That was a typical ploy — putting her in the wrong! She shouldn't even answer him — but she did.

'Not really, no. Darys brought them. I wasn't expecting them, but it was a nice surprise.'

'Yes. I saw how pleased you were. Are you pleased to see me?'

She ignored the last question, her thoughts hooked by the previous statement. 'You saw?' He'd been there, outside, when the others were here! She'd looked . . . but she hadn't seen him! 'Did you follow them? So why didn't you come in while they were here?'

'No, I didn't follow them. They were here when I arrived. I just thought I'd rather see you on your own. That's why I waited until the painter guy went out. Aren't you going to ask me through to the back? I could do with a drink. Or, I know! Let's go to that nice hotel up the road. They've got quite a good menu there. I'll treat you to a meal while we sort out our future.'

Jasmine shook her head to clear her thoughts.

'There's nothing to sort out, Carl. We haven't got a future. Not together.'

'That's what I want to discuss with you. I've seen how popular your café's becoming. I reckon it could support the two of us — if we had the other room through there.' He nodded towards Rhys's gallery. 'I could make that into quite a stylish restaurant and leave you to do the snack-type meals you're doing in here. What d'you say? I reckon I could get eight or ten tables in there. It's completely wasted space, as it is. We could even rent out the walls to him if he wants to continue to display his paintings . . . and get more income that way!'

Jasmine could hardly credit what she was hearing. Her mind flitted back a few phrases.

'You've seen how popular my tea room is?' she queried sharply. 'Over what timescale? The past few hours? A few days? Or a number of weeks?'

She could see that her words had struck home, and she angrily advanced towards him, her finger stabbing the air between them towards his chest.

'Just how close have you been, Carl? Close enough to throw a brick through the window? Close enough to enjoy the sight of a load of manure being dumped on the forecourt? Or close enough to push a live rat through the letterbox?'

Carl backed away as Jasmine advanced, his hand behind him, feeling for the edges of the tables he had to negotiate his way round.

'Eh? You're not blaming that lot on me, Jasmine!'

Jasmine halted, putting her hands on her hips as she eyed him scornfully. 'No? You don't seem overly surprised by what's been happening here!'

'No, well, word drifted through to me after your lodger had been snooping around asking questions about your past.'

'My lodger? I haven't got a lodger! Do you mean Rhys? We're renting separately.' Her brain was whirling round as she spoke almost without thinking. 'What d'you mean, 'snooping around'? Snooping around where?'

'At the hotel, of course. Where else? If you ask me, he's a dodgy character, trying to dig up some dirt on you!'

She stared at him in disbelief. 'But, why would he do that?' Then her eyes narrowed thoughtfully as she recalled what she'd seen in Cardigan a couple of weeks previously. 'When, exactly, are you talking about?'

Carl shrugged. 'How should I know? Fairly recently, I suppose. I didn't exactly see him myself. I'd have told him where to go.' He grinned malevolently. 'And helped him on his way with my fist!'

'What was he asking about?'

'You, of course! Wanting to know about your past. Look, let's discuss it over some food, shall we? Either here or at the hotel, I don't mind which.'

Jasmine felt bewildered. Why had Rhys been to her last place of employment asking about her? She knew he'd been there; she'd seen him with Darys. Was that why he'd taken Darys out for lunch? To ask questions about her? How dare he! He'd no right to go snooping around behind her back.

If he'd wanted to know anything about her, why hadn't he just asked? She felt furious. Just wait till he came back! In fact, she'd deal with it right now while she still felt annoyed.

She stepped nearer to Carl and forcefully hustled him towards the door.

'I'm sorry, Carl. I don't want to have a meal with you, nor a drink. I'd rather you left right away. I've got things to do.'

'Hey, you can't just turn me out!' Carl protested. 'Can't you see? I've come here to help you. We'll make a good team together, you'll see.'

'No, we won't, Carl. I've told you, it's over between us. Now, please go.'

Fortunately, Carl was so taken by surprise at her determination that he leave, that she was able to hustle him through the doorway and close the door behind him before he had made a move to stand his ground. This time, she locked the door and pulled down the blind and hurriedly retreated into her kitchen, ignoring Carl's urgent rapping on the glass.

She quickly rushed upstairs, changed into her trainers, grabbed her bag and hurried downstairs again to the back door. Even if Carl knew about the back lane, she was sure he wouldn't immediately think she intended to leave that way . . . but, for peace of mind, she needed to move quickly.

She swiftly unlocked the door, pulled out the key and slipped outside. Just as swiftly, she replaced the key and locked the door, testing that it was indeed locked. She didn't want Carl, or anyone else, to be able to enter while she was out! Not that she would be long . . . and the way she felt right now, Rhys was as likely to find himself locked out as anyone else!

Eyes alert, she hurried to the end of the lane and edged round the side of the gallery. Carl had taken a couple of steps back from the door and was scrutinising each of the windows in turn, upstairs and down, as if trying to catch a glimpse of her, almost willing her to pass by one the windows.

'In your dreams, boyo!' she breathed, drawing back a little. After a few minutes, during which her heart seemed to be beating fast enough to burst free of her body, she leaned forward again. To her relief, she saw Carl drop his shoulders in defeat, turn away and begin to walk up the road, hopefully towards his car. He showed no signs of glancing back and she decided to risk hurrying across the road, anxious to be on her way. Once safely across, she risked another glance up the road but Carl had gone from her sight.

Right, Rhys Morgan! Watch out! This time, she was going to challenge him face to face.

She'd been to Freshwater Bay before and knew it was about four miles away, but Rhys would have been stopping continually to weigh up different angles and take photographs to reflect on later. She didn't think he would have got very far because he would have followed the cliff tops, whereas she could cut across the headland. Even so, it was over half an hour before she caught sight of him in the distance. He was outlined against the sky overlooking Swanlake Bay. The sight of his lithe movements as he changed position to catch a different angle of light caught at her heartstrings. She really liked him, even when she had thought he might be having a relationship with Darys — and she might have been mistaken about that — and she knew she wanted to know him better, to forge a future with him. But not at the cost of her self-respect.

As she anticipated, he was busy with his camera. She didn't call out to him. He might be precariously balanced and, however annoyed with him she might be, she didn't want to startle him and cause him to fall from the clifftop to the rocky cove below. Consequently, she was only a few yards away from him when he sensed her presence and turned round.

'Oh! Hi!' he greeted her, his face

lighting up. 'You came.'

His greeting was so warmly made that Jasmine nearly lost her resolve to challenge his action in going to Cardigan to check up on her. But she hardened the tender feelings within.

'Yes, I came,' she agreed coolly. 'I had a visitor after you left. Carl, my ex-boyfriend.'

'Oh.' His expression became a bit wary. 'What did he want? He didn't threaten you, did he?' He switched off his camera and jumped down from where he was balanced.

Jasmine stood her ground. 'What makes you think he'd threaten me?'

'Well, I . . . er . . . just put two and two together . . . '

'And went behind my back to question my friends!'

That stopped him. He grimaced wryly. 'He told you, did he? Look, I'm sorry about that.'

'You had no right to question my friends like that! I find it quite offensive.'

'I'm sorry. I thought there might be someone with a grudge against you, and you obviously weren't going to open up. I wanted to help.'

'That still didn't give you the right to go behind my back!'

'No, it didn't. Like I said, I'm sorry. I'm not proud of what I did. Nor about not mentioning it afterwards. I just felt desperate to do something. Not that it got me anywhere. Darys said Carl might think about doing such tricks but didn't think he would actually do them . . . and she didn't think he knew where you had moved to.'

'Well, we were all wrong on that score. I got the feeling he's been here a number of times.'

Her anger with Rhys was fading. Hadn't she herself suspected Carl might be the perpetrator? She had been less than upfront about it . . . and had kept secret the fact that she had seen him and Darys together. Maybe she had better meet him half way?

'I guess I haven't been entirely

honest, either. I saw you in Cardigan with Darys. I thought you were meeting each other behind my back and I . . . well, I've been waiting for an announcement about a blossoming romance between you.'

Rhys's face took on an incredulous expression but, before he could speak, she hurried on, 'If I'd done the right thing and talked about it with either of you — followed you both into the diner there and then instead of running away — you'd have explained why you were there. So, I guess we've both made mistakes.'

Rhys was openly grinning at her. 'You were jealous!'

'No, I wasn't!' Jasmine asserted indignantly, her face flushing pink.

'Yes, you were! Admit it! You were jealous!'

'No, I wasn't,' she said less vehemently. She paused briefly, glancing away, then flicked her eyes back to his. 'Well, okay then, since we're being honest, I was . . . though I expect I'd have got over it . . . eventually!'

Rhys stepped closer and took hold of her hand. He drew her closer, still grinning in triumph.

'Say it properly, then. That you were jealous! Say it!'

'Okay. I was jealous. Will that do?'

'For now. Come here.'

He drew her forward and she went willingly into his arms and, when he lowered his head to hers, she moulded against him, delighting in his kiss, responding fully as his lips parted hers and drank deeply of her.

Jasmine felt weightless. If she had opened her eyes and found she was floating in the sky, she wouldn't have been surprised. It was heavenly. She responded to the force of his passion; searching, testing, enjoying. When they eventually drew apart, Jasmine felt breathless.

'Wow, that was worth waiting for!'

'It was, wasn't it? Let's do it again!' So, they did . . . a few times more.

'We'd best be going back,' Rhys

eventually said. 'I'll pack this up for today. The light's gone, anyway.' He slipped his camera and other artistic materials into his satchel, then reached out to take hold of her hand again.

'I've wanted to kiss you like that for a long time,' he admitted as they began to retrace their way back across the headland, 'but I was scared of frightening you off. I kept thinking you wanted me to, then feeling you retreat from me. It was another reason I wanted to learn a bit about your past. I sensed someone had tried to dominate you — and guessed you needed time to distance yourself from whoever it was. Am I right?'

'Yes.' Jasmine sighed. 'It was Carl, as you've probably guessed . . . or did Darys enlighten you?'

'Only to confirm that I was on the right lines. She said I had to wait until you were ready to tell me yourself.'

So Darys had been a true friend. She was glad of that. It meant a lot to her. Suddenly, she laughed aloud. Rhys looked questioningly at her.

'You know, I came up here spitting fire and brimstone at you! I never thought we'd end up . . . '

' . . . like this,' he finished, slipping his hand around her waist and claiming her lips once more.

It took longer to return home than the outward journey had been. They ran the last few yards along the back lane hand-in-hand like children, laughing together as they paused by the gate, kissing once more. Jasmine felt they were making up for lost time and she revelled in the pulsating joy that surged through her.

Their laughter ceased abruptly when they arrived at the back door. It was almost closed . . . but not quite. Rhys looked questioningly at Jasmine. The fingers of her right hand were splayed across her lips, eyes wide with alarm.

'I locked it!' she whispered.

Rhys reached out and pushed the door open. It swung easily at his touch and he moved forward.

'Stay here,' he commanded Jasmine.

'No.' She clutched at his hand and fearfully followed him inside.

All was quiet. The kitchen door was also ajar and they pushed it open as they moved forward. Nothing seemed amiss and Jasmine found herself relaxing. Maybe she was mistaken? Maybe she had forgotten to lock the door properly in her haste to spit her fury at Rhys? Maybe the lock hadn't engaged properly?

Rhys strode across the kitchen and looked into the tea room.

'It seems okay,' he said over his shoulder. 'It seems it's a false alarm. Let that be a lesson, my girl! Too much anger rots the brain!'

'I was so sure I'd locked it,' Jasmine countered defensively, shaking her head in bewilderment.

'Next time, make sure!'

Though Rhys's words were terse, his tone was light and Jasmine accepted the rebuke.

'I'll put the kettle on,' she volunteered as Rhys continued through the tea room. The temporary fright had taken the shine off their mutual delight in discovering the depth of their feelings for each other, and now she felt subdued. She was taking two mugs from the cupboard when she heard Rhys exclaim aloud.

'What did you say?' she called out.

When Rhys didn't answer, she put the mugs on the table and went through the tea room to where Rhys was still standing on the threshold of his gallery. He seemed frozen in shock and she pushed past him . . . only to halt abruptly at his side.

The gallery was in a shambles. Much of his merchandise had been swept off the shelves and lay broken or in disarray on the floor; paintings had been taken from the walls and flung to the ground . . . and blue paint had been sprayed around at random, disfiguring the walls, floor, ceiling and many of Rhys's paintings.

9

Jasmine wailed. 'Oh, Rhys, I'm so sorry! Who on earth would sink so low as to do something like this? It's dreadful!'

'Well, we don't need too many guesses, do we?' Rhys said bitterly. 'How about your boyfriend, Carl? He makes an ideal suspect, I'd say!'

'Oh!' Her eyes widened in dismay. 'No! He wouldn't! I believed him when he denied doing the other things. I could tell he was speaking the truth. I'm sure of it!'

Rhys raised his right eyebrow. 'I admire your optimism — but I don't share it. He's here. He has the motive. And you gave him the opportunity!'

Jasmine stared at him, aghast at his words. 'Rhys! What are you saying? Are you suggesting I deliberately gave him access to your gallery?'

'No, of course not — not deliberately! But you did leave the door open. I could wring his neck! Just look at it! Wanton destruction!'

'I know . . . but not Carl.' Her voice had lost its certainty, though. She recalled what Carl had said about getting rid of Rhys and taking over the gallery as a restaurant. But it was just talk . . . wasn't it?

But her doubts were flashing across her face as if on a television screen and Rhys didn't miss one of them. He placed his hands gently on her shoulders and regarded her with tenderness.

'I know you don't want to think too badly of him, Jasmine — and it's very loyal of you — but you have to face it. He wants you back and will go to any lengths to destroy what we have going here. Well, he's gone too far this time. I'm reporting it to the police . . . and naming him as chief suspect!'

It was nearly three hours later when the plain-clothes policeman arrived. Rhys and Jasmine had left everything as it was. Jasmine had made a meal for them — a quiche, baked potatoes and some salad — and then got on with some baking for the following day as her stocks had to be constantly replenished, especially after such a busy day as today had been. She chose recipes that she knew well and could do blindfolded if necessary, and the air was filled with the aroma of chocolate sponges, banana and walnut loaves and a couple of moist gingerbreads when the front doorbell pealed.

'Now, Miss Jones, tell me exactly what this young man . . . your ex-boyfriend, I believe? Tell me exactly what he said and did when he called here earlier,' DC Griffiths requested, his notebook at the ready.

Jasmine felt uncomfortable. She knew it looked bad for Carl — and it would look even worse if she repeated, word for word, what Carl had said. On the other hand, she couldn't obstruct the police in their enquiries. She settled for a general outline of what he had said, making more of Carl's longing for her to go back to him and run a restaurant together, and rather less of his specific thought of somehow getting rid of Rhys and converting his gallery into the said restaurant.

'He thought this was an ideal set-up,' she ended. 'I'm sure he'd do nothing to spoil it.'

'Quite,' DC Griffiths murmured non-committally.

'Ideal for whom? You and me — or you and him?' Rhys queried astutely.

'Besides which,' Jasmine said more forcefully, ignoring Rhys's question, 'the more I think about it, the more sure I am that I did lock the back door when I went out. I locked it, and then tested it. You know, shook the door to make sure. So, how would Carl have got inside?'

'But it was unlocked when you returned?' DC Griffiths verified.

'Yes. Unlocked and left ajar . . . as if whoever has done this was taunting us, not even making an effort to leave it as he had found it.'

'But it would have been more puzzling if the door was locked and the damage done inside, wouldn't it? With the door left open, it also leaves the identity of the intruder more open. It could be anyone who happened to see you leave and decided to try his luck. Many incidents like this turn out to be done by an opportunist thief, and thus harder to trace.'

'Yes . . . but it's happened before, hasn't it, Rhys? Someone put a rat in the kitchen, but all the doors were locked.'

DC Griffiths raised an eyebrow. 'A rat in the kitchen? Isn't that stretching it a bit? I mean, rats in a kitchen is a fairly common occurrence, isn't it?'

'Not in my kitchen, it isn't! Not when we'd thoroughly cleaned the place the day before, and there were no places for a rat to squeeze through!'

'Hmm. Anything else? Anything untoward, I mean.'

'Well, there was the brick through the

front window a couple of months back — we reported that to the police — and then a load of manure was dumped on our forecourt.'

'Which of you was that targeted at, do you think?'

Jasmine and Rhys exchanged glances. 'Jasmine, the first; possibly me the second,' Rhys offered.

'Or me again,' Jasmine disagreed. 'In fact, Rhys thought I'd done it to annoy him.'

'Why would he think that? Had you had a row?'

'Not really,' Jasmine admitted, with an embarrassed glance at Rhys. She bit her lower lip, before saying, 'Though I suppose I was a bit upset with him because he'd sketched a portrait of me and then had screwed it up and thrown it in the bin.'

'No,' Rhys corrected. 'I was upset with you because *you* had screwed it up and thrown it in the bin!'

'No, I didn't!' Jasmine argued. 'I found it in the bin. I was nosey and wondered what you'd thrown away. It was a good sketch and I thought you were annoyed with me for . . . ' She flicked an embarrassed glance at DC Griffiths but found him awaiting her answer with an impassive expression. 'You know, for not wanting to, well, form a close relationship with you.'

'And I thought you'd thrown it away for more or less the same reason!' Rhys stated. 'So, if neither you nor I threw it away, who did?'

Jasmine stared at him, the truth slowly impaling itself upon her brain.

'Someone else must have got in! Someone must have a key!' She turned to DC Griffiths. 'So, it can't be Carl, can it?'

'That seems to be so, for that incident, at least,' he agreed. 'But I think we need to keep an open mind on the remaining incidents. For all we know, there may be more than one culprit, so let's keep our options open. Don't you agree, Mr Morgan?'

'Yes, I do.' Rhys glanced apologetically at Jasmine.

'But I locked the door!' Jasmine insisted.

'But you also admitted you were upset,' Rhys pointed out, 'and so you might be mistaken. Look, I'm not saying it is Carl . . . but, as DC Griffiths says, we have to keep him in mind. Whoever has trashed my gallery has done a lot of damage and, even though I might get some of it back in insurance, it will take me months to replace the damaged items.'

'And, I take it, you will be pressing charges?' DC Griffiths clarified.

'Yes.' Again, he glanced apologetically at Jasmine. 'Whoever was responsible, whether Carl or someone else, it was an act of wilful vandalism and deserves to be punished. My livelihood is at stake here.'

'Yes, you're right,' Jasmine agreed. She turned to DC Griffiths. 'Is that all for now? Or have you any more questions?'

'I need the full name and address of the young man in question.'

'He's recently changed his job and moved from where he was living, so the best I can do is give you the name of the hotel where we both worked . . . The Duke Of York in Cardigan.'

'Right. Thank you,' the officer murmured as he wrote in his book. 'Now, I'll take a closer look at the scene of the damage, to be sure nothing has been overlooked, and I'll test for fingerprints, but I don't hold out much optimism on that score. There are too many police dramas on television these days. Even the youngest of criminals know about not leaving any DNA behind to incriminate them. It's only when crimes are unpremeditated that we stand much chance of collecting any viable evidence.'

On that gloomy forecast, DC Griffiths, followed by Rhys, went into the gallery. Jasmine continued her work in the kitchen. By the time DC Griffiths was ready to depart, her cakes were cooling on racks and she had a few fresh scones ready to butter for immediate consumption.

Ten minutes later, DC Griffiths gave them an incident number for future reference and took his leave, wiping the crumbs from around his mouth.

'I advise you both to get a burglar alarm system installed as soon as possible,' were his parting words. 'There's nothing like a loud strident noise to scare away the would-be miscreants, in case it should happen again!'

Rhys and Jasmine agreed, though it seemed a bit too late to give them any present benefit.

'Did he say we could tidy it up now?' Jasmine asked, as she carried the used plates to the sink. 'Maybe it won't be as bad as it looks when we sort through everything.'

'It's pretty bad, though there are some things I can probably salvage. I'm going to take photos of everything to send to my insurers first. Are you sure you want to help? It's getting quite late.'

'All the more reason for me to help. I'll get some bin liners for anything beyond hope.'

'Don't start until I've cleared a path to tread. I'll fetch in the long-handled brush to sweep up the broken glass,' Rhys said, heading to the back door. 'This could take some time.'

* * *

It was past midnight when they called a halt. After photographing the scene from a few different angles, Rhys swept the broken glass into heaps to be shovelled up and put into stout bags. Jasmine threw all damaged items into another bag and put those she thought undamaged together on the cleared counter. Once the floor was clear, Rhys set about restoring his shelving to order and then began to lift his paintings down from their positions on the walls. Every one of them had some paint sprayed on them, though with different degrees of damage.

'I can paint over the oils and acrylics,' Rhys murmured thoughtfully, holding them up to assess the damage on each individual picture, 'though most will need reframing. There's enough to keep me busy for a quite a while, that's for sure. Let's just stack them over here to clear the main wall. I'll repaint that tomorrow. At least we kept the paint we had left over when we were decorating.'

They worked on for a while longer but, at last, Rhys reckoned they'd done all they could for that night. He put his hands on Jasmine's waist and drew her closer.

'I'm truly sorry about all this. I know it's been hard for you. I hope it's not Carl. I just can't be as sure about that as you are, since I don't know the guy.' He hesitated, studying her upturned face. He seemed as if he was going to say something else, but thought better of it. His expression relaxed and he said lightly, 'Thanks for helping. What a day, eh?'

He's right about that, Jasmine silently agreed. Emotion-wise, it had been quite a rollercoaster — and physically demanding as well. She seemed to sense that Rhys had withdrawn from her . . . from that wonderful, heady euphoria that had swept them into each other's arms up on the headland. She wondered what Rhys had been going to say. Was he blaming her for her connection with Carl? Was he thinking that, but for her, his paintings would still be intact? If Carl was to blame, his resentment would be justified . . . but she still hoped Carl was innocent. Was she being foolishly loyal? Was that what Rhys didn't like, the fact that she was still feeling loyal towards Carl? Or was it simply that he didn't believe she no longer cared for Carl? But it was the truth.

Her lips tingled with longing. She wanted him to gather her into his arms and smother her face with kisses. She contemplated taking the initiative — but dreaded being rejected, repelled even. So, instead, she stretched up on her toes and briefly kissed him on his lips.

'Carl means nothing to me emotionally,' she said quietly as she stood back. 'It's been over between us for a long time — on my part, anyway. But that doesn't mean I have to see him totally as Mr Bad Guy, even though I don't even like him any more.'

She looked at him quizzically, awaiting his response.

Rhys nodded. 'You're right, I know.'

He kissed her lightly. Their passionate feelings up on the headland had been overwhelmed by the break-in and both of them were too emotionally drained to resurrect them at this late hour.

'Let's call it a day.'

He dropped his forehead to touch hers and nibbled at her lips when she lifted her head slightly, but made no move to go further.

Jasmine understood. She, too, was tired. She just hoped their embryonic relationship would survive the incident.

She didn't sleep well, and Rhys was already painting over the walls of the gallery when she sleepily made her way downstairs the following day. Later, after they had eaten breakfast, Rhys looked in the local directory to find some firms who specialised in fitting burglar alarms and changing locks.

'We'd better get in touch with Lona before we go ahead,' he cautioned. 'After all, it's her property and she may pay part of the cost.'

However, when he telephoned Lona's phone number, all he got was her answering machine.

'I left a message saying what we're wanting to do and the reasons why,' he told Jasmine. 'I'm sure she'll get back to us as soon as she can. In the meantime, let's go ahead and get some details, anyway. No-one is going to be able to come immediately, so we may as well get as far as we can.'

Jasmine agreed, especially about getting the lock changed. When they were still only getting Lona's answer-phone later on in the day, they decided to go ahead and arranged to have the lock on the back door changed the following day. In the meantime, Rhys continued to get his gallery back into order and started renovating some of his paintings.

'Why don't you prop your undamaged paintings around my walls?' Jasmine suggested. 'You might get some extra sales that way.'

She was pleased when Rhys agreed. She felt in some way responsible for the perpetrator getting access to Rhys's gallery, even though she was one hundred per cent certain she had locked the back door. She kept him plied with refreshments in between serving her own customers and the coolness that had been between them at the beginning of the day warmed somewhat, especially when, just before lunchtime, she darted in to tell him he had a customer for one of his watercolours.

Mid-afternoon, a young woman having afternoon tea hesitantly asked about the card in the window advertising for a waiter or waitress.

'Is the position still open?' she asked.

'Yes, it is,' Jasmine assured her. 'Are you interested?'

'Yes . . . if the hours are suitable.'

Jasmine quickly explained the hours she needed and the sort of duties she required of whoever got the job. 'It's not full-time yet,' she explained. 'Business is building up nicely and I'm sure I will be able to offer more hours as the season gets on its way.'

'That's fine,' the woman agreed. 'I live locally and I'll be able to feel my way into it this way. My name's Anwen, by the way. Shall I get some references and bring them in tomorrow?'

That was agreed, and Jasmine felt it was a step forward. If only Rhys hadn't had the setback, she would have been ecstatic. As it was, although the atmosphere was once again friendly between them, neither felt able to resume the newfound closeness they had experienced up on the headland.

They still hadn't heard from Lona by the end of the day.

'I'll sleep in my sitting room with the middle door open,' Rhys decided. 'No one is going to get in again!'

There were no disturbances during the night. Even so, they were both much relieved when the locksmith came just before lunchtime and changed the lock on the back door. They were given three keys; one each, and one to keep in a safe place.

'And, if we don't go out that way when we leave the place empty, we can also draw the bolts across,' Rhys commented. 'We've got to be security-conscious from now on.'

Jasmine wondered whether he was making a subtle dig at her, but she decided not to rise to it. After all, it was his part of the property that had suffered the vandalism.

Anwen popped in with two character reference letters, from the local vicar and Margaret at the post office.

'Right! Why don't you start tomorrow?' Jasmine suggested. 'Then you'll be settled in by Saturday. We always have more customers at the weekend.'

With the problem of getting extra help solved, Jasmine went to bed with a lighter heart and quickly fell asleep. When she awakened suddenly some time later, she couldn't think what had disturbed her. She lay still, listening intently. Had there been a noise of some sort? She couldn't hear anything, apart from the thudding of her racing heart. After a moment or two, she settled back but didn't immediately drop off to sleep.

Maybe a trip to the bathroom would help her settle again. She swung her legs out of bed. All was quiet as she padded down the stairs but, as she turned towards the bathroom, she heard a sound at the rear door . . . as if someone had dropped a bunch of keys.

Her body froze. There was someone there!

She took a step nearer, just as whoever was outside straightened up and a distorted image was outlined through the obscure glass. It was a man, she was sure . . . quite a large man, at that. As her breath caught in her throat, the man pressed his face against the glass, squashing his features.

Whether it was because he had seen her and wished to frighten her, or in order to see more clearly into the passage, Jasmine didn't know — but the effect was so alarming that she screamed involuntarily, loud and prolonged.

10

As Jasmine's scream echoed through the air, Rhys hurtled down the stairs, his trousers dangling from one hand.

'What's the matter?' he asked, swiftly reaching her side and putting his arms protectively around her.

'There's a man outside!' Jasmine hissed. 'He was trying to get in!'

'Right! Let me get at him!'

As he hopped from one foot to the other, hastily dragging on his jeans over his pyjama bottoms, Jasmine took the key off its hook at the top of the door and fitted it into the lock. She could no longer see the man through the glass panel in the door and there were sounds of some sort of scuffle taking place in the back yard.

Rhys roughly pulled her aside and plunged into the yard. Two men, one much larger than the other, were struggling together. Rhys's uncertainty over which of the men he should try to restrain was settled for him when the larger man floored his opponent with a hefty blow to the side of his head. He fell to the ground, and the other fled down the path towards the back gate.

As Rhys briefly hovered over the prone figure, the fallen man lifted his head. 'Don't bother with me! It's the other one! Get after him! Stop him!'

Was he telling the truth? Rhys didn't know. But his heart was pounding and he felt a force of anger towards whoever had wantonly destroyed much of his work — and caused the other problems between him and Jasmine — and, if this was the same man, he was going to do his best to find out what was behind it all.

He took off after the fleeing man, barely hearing, and certainly not taking in, Jasmine's startled exclamation of, 'Carl! What are you doing here?'

It was dark, but not too dark to see the larger man turn left out of the small yard and hurry away down the back lane towards the road. The man had a slight head start, but Rhys was more agile and was only a few strides behind him by the time the man rushed round the corner onto the main road. Rhys immediately realised the man was heading towards a van parked across the road. Another few strides, and he was on to him.

Rhys grabbed hold of his shoulder and pulled him backwards, determined not to let him escape. The man swung around and aimed a blow at him, catching the side of his head. Dazed, Rhys stepped back but reached out again as the man yanked open the driver's door. This time, he managed to land a blow himself before the man thumped him in his midriff, taking the breath out of his lungs.

Rhys staggered backwards but, with the adrenalin flowing through him, he wasn't about to give up so easily. He reached forward again as the man scrambled into the driver's seat and, wedging himself against the open door, he tried to pull the man out of the vehicle.

He was aware that someone had come to his aid and was trying to grab hold of the man's arm, but the space was too confined for the two of them to manoeuvre together. As they struggled to detain the would-be burglar, the man managed to start the engine and, regardless of the fact that the van door was open and the two men still holding onto his sleeve, he slammed into first gear and the van jerked forward, dragging Rhys with it.

As Rhys was jerked forward, he heard Jasmine scream his name. At the same time, he felt strong hands around his body pulling him backwards.

'Don't be a fool! Let him go!' the man at his side yelled in his ear.

Rhys had no option but to obey. He was already staggering forward with the motion of the van and it was gaining in speed. As he let go, his feet went from under him and he crashed to the ground. He felt the arms around him pulling him backwards away from the van's wheels and the two of them rolled across the road in a locked embrace, coming to a stop by the opposite kerb.

'Rhys! Rhys! Are you all right? Are you hurt? You could've been killed!'

It was Jasmine's voice and he opened his eyes.

'What do you think you were doing?' she screamed, dropping at his side and pummelling her fists against his chest. 'You crazy mutt! You could have been killed, for Heaven's sake!'

Her voice ended with a sob and Rhys realised that tears were running down her cheeks. He forced a grin. 'Glad to know you care! But lay off the fisticuffs, eh? I feel a bit tender there.'

'Oh, Rhys, I'm sorry! Are you all right? Can you stand up? Help him, Carl. Get hold of his other arm!'

Carl? This other man was Carl? His brain back-tracked about five minutes. Yes, he'd heard Jasmine say something about Carl as he ran after the intruder.

He struggled to sit up and looked at his rival suspiciously.

'So you're Carl.' He narrowed his eyes. 'Where do you come into this?'

He levered himself up, shrugging off Jasmine's hand under his arm.

Carl backed off a pace, his hands held out, palms upward. 'Hey! I came to help. I know you thought I was part of all the aggravation you've been having, but I'm not!'

'Then what are you doing here? It's two or three o'clock in the morning! Not exactly the normal hour for a social visit.'

'How about, 'Thanks for saving my neck'?' Carl suggested with the hint of a sneer.

'Yeah, well . . . thanks,' Rhys muttered ungraciously. 'But you've not answered my question.'

'Look, let's get back inside, eh?' Jasmine suggested, fearing that the aggressive stance of the two men might flare into battle. 'I locked the back door but I'd be happier if we were on the inside, not standing out here.'

The two men glared at each other but acquiesced as Jasmine determinedly stalked back up the lane to their back gate. She felt shaken by the force of her anguish when she thought Rhys was going to be dragged along the road as the intruder made his getaway. It left her trembling and she wanted to bury herself in his arms and feel the reassurance of his strong body against hers. But how could she, when Carl, her ex-boyfriend, was present and mainly responsible for saving him? And Rhys didn't seem to want any demonstration of her feelings. A glance over her shoulder showed the two men were totally ignoring each other as they followed in her wake.

Once back inside, Jasmine put the kettle on and the two men sat at the table, on opposite sides. Men! She slid a plate of biscuits between them.

'Have a cookie,' she suggested, 'while we decide what to do. I mean, should we report it to the police?'

'We'd better, since we reported the other incidents,' Rhys decided. 'But I'd still like to know your part in it all,' he added, glaring at Carl again.

Carl helped himself to a biscuit, which he dunked in his mug of coffee before replying. 'Like I explained to Jaz earlier, I thought I'd stick around and watch out for another attack on your property. I thought whatever the guy was up to, he wouldn't stop until he'd succeeded, and it looks like I was right! Who was the guy? Did either of you recognise him?'

'I didn't get a good look at him, except for his distorted image through the glass,' Jasmine excused herself. 'And that was horrifying!' she recalled, shuddering at the memory. 'The hammered glass made him look like a monster!' She shuddered again. 'What about you, Rhys?'

'I don't know him, but I'd recognise him again. Hang on! I'll get my sketch pad.'

He slipped out through the door and

crossed the passageway into his sitting room, returning with his sketch pad and pencil. Engrossed in recalling his memory, he made a quick sketch, adding a few lines here and there, smudging some lines with the edge of his thumb to give depth to the sketch.

'What d'you think?' he asked Carl, tilting the sketch towards him.

'Yeh, that's him,' Carl agreed, 'but who is he? Why is he targeting the pair of you? What's he after?'

'That's the million-dollar question!' Rhys murmured.

'Right! Well, I think it's about time I went,' Carl responded, 'and I think you should come with me, Jaz. It's not safe for you here.'

Jasmine shook her head. 'I'm not going anywhere. Whoever he is, he's not driving me out of my home and business.'

'He might come back.'

'He won't get in. Besides, he now knows his key won't fit.'

'You would still be safer with me!'

Rhys stood up. 'I'll leave you to sort it out between you. Goodnight . . . and, er, thanks for your help,' he directed at Carl as he left the kitchen.

Jasmine and Carl stood in silence as they heard Rhys's footsteps go up the stairs. Jasmine spoke first.

'I'm staying here, Carl. This is where I belong, now. I appreciate what you did tonight, but it doesn't change things between us. It's over. I've moved on. You need to move on, too.'

'Huh! It'll never work between you. He doesn't care about you like I do.'

Jasmine shrugged. She didn't know what Rhys felt for her at the moment. 'Maybe you're right. I don't know . . . but it doesn't change things. I'm staying here. I'll see you out, shall I?'

She headed for the door into the tea room, to show him out that way, but Carl didn't step aside to allow her to pass in front him as she expected him to do. Instead, he pulled her into his arms and kissed her fiercely on her lips. For a moment, she was stunned and froze in his arms.

'Jasmine, I just thought . . . ' Rhys's voice came from the other door. 'Oh, sorry! I didn't mean to disturb you. I just wanted to make sure all the outer doors were locked . . . if you decided to go with Carl.'

Jasmine pushed away Carl's arms, furious with him for forcing a kiss on her . . . and furious with herself for not pulling free sooner.

'I'm staying here!' she snapped. 'Carl's just leaving. You can lock up after him! I'm going back to bed!'

And she stalked back upstairs to her room, leaving the two men to sort themselves out.

* * *

Both of them were tired when they came down to breakfast the following day. There was no time for a lie-in. Customers would be arriving soon after nine o'clock and Jasmine wanted to be ready for them.

Anwen arrived just before nine and Jasmine explained which bread rolls to be making up in readiness for their first customers. Meanwhile, Rhys telephoned the police to report the overnight incident. They accepted the verbal report and didn't think it necessary to send anyone out. When Rhys mentioned the sketch he had made, the duty sergeant suggested Rhys drop it off at the police station within the next few days. Rhys agreed.

Later, just when the tea room was full of customers having morning coffee or ordering various take-aways, Rhys popped his head round the kitchen door.

'Just had a phone call from Lona,' he reported.

'Oh, good! Take these out to table four, Anwen . . . and these for table six,' handing her a tray, following her into the tea room with the other and placing it on the counter. She returned to Rhys. 'What did she say?'

'She's been away for a few days

visiting her sister and got back last night. She said it's okay about changing the back door lock and she'll come round this afternoon to discuss the burglar alarm. I said I'd go to Tenby to collect her but she said the bus is handy, so I'll get back to my gallery.'

Jasmine was pleased about that. They hadn't seen Lona since she'd had the tea room up and running, so it would be nice to let her see how it was beginning to thrive. Rhys had successfully painted over the sprayed paint on the walls of his gallery, had a reasonable display on show, and was busy repairing the display shelves. If only they could sort out why they were being targeted by the unknown vandal, all would be hunky-dory for them!

The answer came from an unexpected quarter. Lona arrived as promised soon after two o'clock and, after admiring the set-up of the tea room and then Rhys's gallery, where she bought one of his paintings of Manorbier Castle, she settled down on the sofa in Rhys's sitting room while Jasmine made up a tray of tea, scones and biscuits.

As Jasmine pushed open the door with her hip and carried the tray to place it on the coffee table, she heard Lona say, 'That sketch you were telling me about, Rhys — it's not this one, is it?'

Jasmine glanced at her and was astonished to see how pale her face was. The sketch was shaking in her hand.

Rhys nodded. 'Yes, that's it,' he confirmed. 'I'm going to drop it off at the police station when I take you back to Tenby later on this afternoon. Why? Do you know him?'

Lona seemed to sink within herself. She was clutching the sketch so tightly her knuckles were white and she was in danger of tearing the paper. She sank back against the cushion.

'It's Eryl, my son,' she almost whispered. 'I'm so sorry! I should have known he wouldn't take it lying down.'

Both Jasmine and Rhys stared at her in amazement.

'Your son?' Jasmine echoed. 'But . . . why?'

Lona took a deep breath. 'He wanted to open a betting shop here in Manorbier. That's what he does, you know. He runs a chain of betting shops. Oh, it's all quite legal and above board . . . but I didn't want there to be one in Manorbier. I thought it would spoil the village. That's why I decided to rent the property out instead of selling it. That way, I could keep control of what businesses were run here. Oh, my dears, I'm so sorry he's been causing all your upsets. He was hoping to drive you out, of course . . . hoping I would be too discouraged to try to rent again and would let him have it. I wouldn't, of course! I'd have found some way to stop him! Can you ever forgive me?'

There were tears in her eyes. Jasmine flopped down on the sofa beside her and put her arms around her.

'There's nothing to forgive you for,' she assured her. 'It wasn't your doing.' She looked up at Rhys. 'But what are we going to do? We've involved the police.'

Rhys took hold of Lona's hands. 'We'll drop all charges, Lona . . . but he has got to stop. He's got to leave our businesses alone.'

Lona shook her head. 'No! He's quite ruthless. He has put other people out of business — smaller bookmakers; owners of properties he wanted who wouldn't sell to him at the price he was prepared to offer; waiting until they were desperate to sell and then offering even less.' She looked from one to the other of them, her eyes sad but her mouth determined. 'No, you must go ahead. He'll only get what he deserves . . . and I must make sure he doesn't get his hands on this property, even when I'm gone.'

She put down the sketch and visibly pulled herself together. 'Now, I'll have that cup of tea, Jasmine dear . . . and then, Rhys, if you will take me back to Tenby, I will make an appointment to see my solicitor as soon as possible.

Today, if he's available. The sooner I sort this out, the better!'

As she left, she took Jasmine's hands. 'You're both doing very well here . . . better even than I dared hope. I knew you both had it in you when I first saw you.' She smiled and added, 'And, once this is settled, you and Rhys will be able to sort other things out, too.'

On that enigmatic note, she got into Rhys's van and was driven away.

The next few hours were too busy for Jasmine to give her words more than a fleeting thought, and she didn't repeat them to Rhys when he returned. They had had enough false starts to a romance between them, without rushing into something at someone else's instigation!

Over the next few weeks, Lona's solicitor drew up an extremely generous repayment plan for Rhys and Jasmine to become joint owners of the property, with their businesses kept as separate identities. Lona also generously stood as guarantor for the payments with their banks.

'You are an extremely fortunate young lady,' Mr Pritchard assured Jasmine when the proposal was put to him.

Jasmine couldn't agree more.

Eryl Hughes was charged with various offences and was freed on bail until he was called to trial. He was forbidden to visit Manorbier in any circumstances and was assured that he would be held responsible for any acts of retaliation against his mother, Rhys or Jasmine and any such acts would be added to the charges already held against him.

* * *

By the end of the season, Rhys and Jasmine had both established their businesses on a firm footing. Visitors dwindled to a trickle towards the end of September and they decided to shorten the hours of opening throughout the winter months — even having days off together, when Anwen and another local lady served a restricted menu and sold goods from the gallery.

On one such day, when a wintry sun hung pink in the sky, Jasmine and Rhys packed a lunch, some drawing materials and a paperback novel into their haversacks and trekked along the cliff top to Swanlake Bay.

'We have some unfinished business to complete here,' Rhys smiled, drawing Jasmine into his arms when they reached the headland.

'We do?' Jasmine queried, her heart beating rapidly.

'Yes. I remember kissing a bewitching woman here a few months ago, intending to ask her to be my girl . . . but events conspired against me.'

'Well, we did have a lot of things to sort out, and get our businesses established,' Jasmine murmured, her heart beating erratically . . . or was it Rhys's heart she could feel beating against her own?

'That's true! But now, I think it's time to put other things on a firmer footing; don't you?'

'Mmm. This 'ravishing, bewitching girl' — you haven't been playing fast and loose with me, have you? What does she look like? Is she pretty?'

'Usually . . . though, at the moment, I admit she has very red cheeks and a bright red nose!'

'Oh . . . you . . . ' Jasmine grinned and playfully pushed at his chest, but Rhys stood firm. 'So, you didn't fall for her looks, then?'

'Oh, I don't know! She fairly knocked me for six when I first saw her,' Rhys admitted. He searched back in his memory to that day in spring. 'The breeze was blowing through her hair and I wanted to twist my fingers through her curls . . . like this.'

He reached out and gently pulled out a curl and let it re-curl around his first finger. Holding it captive by his thumb, he drew her face towards his.

Jasmine didn't resist. Her lips parted

slightly, tingling in anticipation. Rhys's lips felt like velvet as they caressed hers and she rose up on her toes to enjoy his touch more, her fingers entwining in his hair.

When they drew apart, Rhys ran the backs of his fingers down her cheek until he could cup the tip of her chin between his thumb and first finger.

'So?' he breathed softly.

'So . . . what?' she echoed, just as softly.

'How about it? Will you be my girl?'

Jasmine sighed with pure pleasure. She thought about teasing him further . . . but they had waited long enough for this moment.

'Yes,' she breathed.

'I mean forever.' Rhys qualified his question.

Jasmine beamed. 'For ever and ever.'

And they kissed again.

Books by Karen Abbott
in the Linford Romance Library:

RED ROSE GIRL
SUMMER ISLAND
A TIME TO FORGIVE
LOVE IS BLIND
LOVE CONQUERS ALL
A MATTER OF TRUST
DESIGNS FOR LOVE
WHEN TRUE LOVE WINS
A TASTE OF HAPPINESS
THE HEART KNOWS NO BOUNDS
THE TURNING TIDE
OUTRAGEOUS DECEPTION
RISING TO THE CALL
A FRENCH MASQUERADE
A HEART DIVIDED
DANGER COMES CALLING
TO FACE THE PAST
DANGEROUS INTRIGUE
JUST A SUMMER ROMANCE
AN UNSUITABLE ALLIANCE
HER RELUCTANT HEART
AFRAID TO LOVE
TO CAPTURE A HEART

FAITH FOR THE FUTURE
A CHANGE OF HEART
ILLUSIONS OF LOVE
A DIVIDED INHERITANCE
ELUSIVE LOVE
THE FARRINGTON FORTUNE
A BRIDE FOR LORD MOUNTJOY

Other titles in the
Linford Romance Library:

CYPRUS DREAM

Sheila Holroyd

Lorna had come to Cyprus reluctantly, as her aunt's holiday companion. There she met James, who helped her to find out that there was more to the island than hotels and beaches. But could he save her when a ruthless scheme to exploit the island's beauty put her in deadly danger? What would happen to their growing friendship when the holiday was over? And what were her aunt's secret plans?

CHATEAU OF THE NYMPH

Sheila Daglish

When Jenna goes to work in her aunt's French hotel, she finds that someone is determined to force her family out. Is it the darkly forbidding Luc de Villiers? Centuries ago, the son of the lord of the chateau had fallen in love with the girl from the village inn. Was history repeating itself? Only when Jenna's life is put in danger does she discover the truth behind the chateau's legend and find love in place of long-ago tragedy.

LORD ATHERTON'S WARD

Fenella Miller

When their father, Sir John, dies leaving Sarah Ellison and her younger sister Jane orphaned, his choice of guardian is entirely disagreeable to Sarah — particularly with Lord Atherton's insistence that they leave their family home and move to Highfield Hall to remain under the care of his mother. The young, passionate Sarah refuses to bow down to the command of anyone — but will her headstrong behaviour alienate Lord Atherton, or prove that she is a girl he can respect?

COTTAGE IN THE COUNTRY

Wendy Kremer

Amy inherits Rose Cottage, which is in a terrible state of repair. However, wanting to gain a share of its value, her relatives hope that she will refuse the bequest. But Amy keeps Rose Cottage, employing local architect Ben to overhaul the building. Despite living amid chaos during the transformation Amy is determined to stay. If only she could include Ben permanently in her life things would be perfect — but she's not the only one who likes Ben . . .

FOLLIES HOTEL

Anne Holman

When Julianne's engagement ring goes missing and her love letters disappear, she is distraught. Then she hears that her beloved fiancé, the Earl of Featherstonhaugh, is involved in scandal. When he stops writing to her, Julianne decides she must find out what has happened. She goes to his London house and discovers the embarrassing reason . . . Can their true love overcome the difficulty?

CHLOE'S FRIEND

Valerie Holmes

Miss Chloe Branton has been found a position as a laundry maid in a wealthy country house. Although she dislikes the life, she respects her father's wishes, knowing the position will be temporary. Chloe has been placed there for her own safety — where the master of the house watches her. When she needs the help of the man she is falling in love with, Chloe does not know whether Mr Tobias Poole will betray her or be her friend . . .